A Long Night in Codroy

A Long Night in Codroy

Donald G. Dodds

Breakwater
100 Water Street
P.O. Box 2188
St. John's, Newfoundland
A1C 6E6

Canadian Cataloguing in Publication Data

Dodds, Donald G.

A long night in Codroy

ISBN 1-55081-006-5

1. Dodds, Donald G. 2. Game wardens—Newfoundland—Biography. I. Title.

SK354.D62A3 1991 639.9'092 C91-097711-9

Cover Photo: *Johnny Fox, Donald Dodds*

TO PEARL

Contents

In The Beginning 9

Part I - Yarns About People 13

Dreams and Yarns 15

Obseet 16

Jim Barlow 25

Dear Folks—Excerpts From Pearl's Letters Home 34

A Long Night In Codroy 42

New Car 63

Part II - Yarns From the Outports 69

The Sea 71

The *Maude Best* 72

Oderin 80

A Little Blue Mitt 88

Part III - If It's Good For A Scoff 99

Animals and People 101

Rangifer 102

Beoth 116

Dear Folks—Excerpts From Pearl's Letters Home 122

Guashawit 128

If It's Good For A Scoff 136

You Can Never Step Twice In The Same River . .158

In The Beginning

"How would you like to take on a goose project in Newfoundland?" Ollie asked.

Dr. Oliver (Ollie) Hewitt had summoned me to his office one April morning in 1953 and, as I stood trying to think about geese and Newfoundland after he spoke, he said, "I've got to call St. John's tomorrow with an answer, so why don't you talk it over with Pearl tonight and let me know in the morning."

"When would I be going?" I asked hesitantly, still not comprehending what it was all about.

"Oh, in two or three weeks," Ollie said matter of factly. "I'll look after getting your final exams made up for you early. Don't worry about that."

Pearl and I did discuss it that night and made one of those rare, hasty decisions in life that was a right one. The next morning I went straight to Ollie's office at eight o'clock and announced, almost confidently, that I was prepared to head for Newfoundland to work on the goose project.

"Not goose, dummy," Ollie exclaimed, "moose!"

So it was that I did go in 1953 and again in 1954 and studied moose with Doug Pimlott. In 1955 Pearl and I moved to Newfoundland and while there we wrote both letters home and a few stories of people and animals. Some of the stories were published later and the credits are noted here.

Recently we came upon some of our letters, published and unpublished scribbles from the 50s, and decided to bring them together in this little book. There is a common thread throughout the make-believe and the real life we wrote about that ties each person to a natural world, with the possible exception of Bouche. His is more of a personal struggle in adjusting to a changing world. Bouche reflects a somewhat different image from the others, but the name is, nevertheless, a valid reflection of a life in Newfoundland in 1955.

In "Yarns About People" the focus is on those who have lived away from the sea for much of their lives. Beginning with the Beothuk, where the tie with a natural world was almost complete, we move through four different glimpses of life in the 1950s when the Island began a shocking change towards modernity—with such things as roads and cars for Bouche to ponder and government assistance for Jim to drink from. Pearl's letters in this part and in Part III are both glimpses of people and reflections of Newfoundland life from a 'wildlifer's' wife who was living in what was, to her, a new and wondrous setting.

"Yarns From The Outports" reflects more closely what many North Americans understand about Newfoundland, perhaps. That is, a people's dependency on the sea and all it provided; the turrs and cod and caplin, lobster, halibut, ducks and bull birds. Some were caught by jigging and some were shot on swatches from behind ballicater. It was all there and, by adding a few rabbits taken in slips and sticks cut for firewood and fencing and blue potatoes and turnip from a tiny garden amongst the rocks and sod, you had it all. Or almost, anyway. Since my travels often took me by coastal boat and dory I had a chance to stay with many friends in the outports. In their homes, I heard dozens of yarns over tea and cribbage and a few of them are repeated here.

"If It's Good For A Scoff" reflects more of a people's attitude toward wild things than how they lived with the natural world. Sometimes there was a belief in an everlasting supply and sometimes, if the animal really was known to be no longer present, there was a belief in its eventual return. Sometimes there was fear, too, as in the case of bears, but always there were two very strong feelings reflected. The other was a strong utilitarian belief that if it was good for a scoff, kill it and eat it.

The following are the real people in these stories and narratives. Some are alive but many are dead. They are: Sheila Hall, Stevie Hall, Steve Hall, Margaret Hall, Selby Moss, Art Taylor, Edith Taylor, Doug Pimlott (Mrs. O'Quinn), (Mrs. Hillier), Eric Johnston, Eileen Johnston, Jean Hall, Heber and Dorothy Roberts, (Mrs.

White), Gerry Mercer, Dorothy Roberts, Bill Cormier, Jim Collier, Cp. John Hogan, Cst. Wayne Porter, Cst. Roger Haddad, Harold Guzzwell, Gus Roberts, Capt. Harry Walters, Jack Saunders, Uncle Bren Tilley, Bob Folker, Clarence Elms, Gordie Butt, Ron Hounsell, Magistrate Jack White, Dave Pike, Eldon Pace, Dr. Byrne, Dr. Bob Dove, Ron Callahan, John 'Jack' Nichols and Art Butt. All the rest of the names appearing are totally fictitious and any resemblance to any person, living or dead, is accidental.

"Obseet" was originally published in the Blossom Edition of *The Kentville Advertiser,* while "The *Maude Best*" previously appeared as "The Queen Maude" in *The Atlantic Advocate*. Both are published here by permission. "Beoth," "Guashawit" and "Rangifer" were taken from the author's book *Wild Captives,* published by MacMillan of Canada and St. Martin's Press (1965).

Part I

Yarns About People

Dreams and Yarns

Some of these stories are true but most are not. Most are just dreams or yarns. There were wonderful yarners in Newfoundland and I cannot begin to do them justice. Still, I wanted to tell these few stories to you and, in the course of doing so, to remember a few good friends. In these five stories, entitled "Yarns About People," Newfoundland friends remembered are Harry Walters, Doug Pimlott, Steve and Margaret Hall, Stevie and Sheila, Heber Roberts, Art and Edith Taylor, Skipper Jim Collier, Mrs. White, Gerry Mercer, John Hogan, Wayne Porter, Roger Haddad, Eric Johnston, Harold Guzzwell, Gus Roberts, Max Rabbits and Pearl and Whiskey the dog. Many of them are dead now, but they are still friends. All the other characters named are, of course, fictitious and any resemblance to any person living or dead other than those names above is both unintentional and accidental.

Obseet

The first humans known to have lived on the Island of Newfoundland for certain were Beothuks and much of what has been written of them has apparently been less than accurate. Fred Rowe, in his *Extinction, The Beothuks of Newfoundland* takes some authors to task for capitalizing "...on this (Beothuk) mythology, building up its dramatic and sentimental aspects...." He takes particularly direct aim at those who painted (European) Newfoundlanders as people who may have "murdered for fun."

Cultural assimilation and change occur slowly between ethnic groups over time at points of contact where cultures interrelate. During the several hundred years of European exploration and colonization, hundreds of cultural shocks reverberated between indigenous people and visitors to their lands. Europeans, following earlier Arab practices, used African tribes that practised slavery to help them introduce slaves into their own economies and in North America indigenous tribes often captured and enslaved other native people to provide seasonal labour. Stealing, warfare, murder and slavery were present in this land long before the Europeans settled here. These are behaviours common to the human race and may often be a function of both culture and economics. Europeans, however, did introduce a new and sometimes brutal measure of competition for land and resources as well as a market economy that helped to alter the behaviour of Indians toward both animals and plants. Europeans also introduced diseases for which the Indian lacked natural defenses and, through trade, they introduced dietary changes that for certain people, especially the meat eaters, signalled disaster.

When I first examined the Beothuk literature in St. John's Gosling Library in the 1950s, I admit to having been transported back to a childhood when I searched longingly for evidence of the past in Iroquois country. At that time I had romanticized the Five (later Six) Nations, their government, their agriculture, their raids and colonization of new lands to the west and north. Now I allowed myself to romanticize the native North American again, this time the Red Indian of Newfoundland. I wrote "Obseet," a romantic myth and I chose a Beothuk Spirit as a messenger for a utopian dream. Yet, in doing so, I tried not to consider the conflict of cultures which lay at the heart of the Beothuk demise. I invite you to meet *Obseet*, eternal caretaker of the Beothuk flame, in a dream of Newfoundland we should not lose.

❧

Every night of every year, just at dusk, a campfire kindles in the country of *Mogazeesh*. It burns during rain, snow and wind all through the hours of darkness and with the first ray of dawn it is gone. No coals or ashes are ever left. Even as you stand on the site you cannot tell that a fire has burned before, beneath your feet. The fire may kindle anywhere in the country where the *Mogazeesh* have journeyed, but most often it burns about the great water Beothuk or along the banks of the *Shebon*, a river which carries the Beothuk water to the sea.

If ever you may be fortunate to camp at the exact spot where the Beothuk spirit of *Boobeeshawt* is to burn at dark, you will need to make no fire yourself, for though wood is never added, the fire burns with great heat. Heat to boil a kettle and provide you warmth. Some have seen this fire, but spoken to no one, for it is better to be content in the knowledge of a secret truth than to bear the jibes of the unbelievers. There is something else those who have witnessed this fire have seen and heard as well. This is the friendly *Mogazeesh*, called *Obseet*, the eternal caretaker of the Beothuk flame. Out of the curling wood smoke the graceful body of the Red Indian Boy emerges soon after the beginning of the first glow of the blaze. In winter *Obseet* wears the skin of *Kosweet*, the caribou, and *Mamshet*, the beaver, with the furside close to his body, but during the summer he wears the fur of these creatures outside with the leather next to his skin. On the very warmest of days, he wears only a skirt-like wrap from waist to knees and moosins made from *Kosweet*.

To camp at this one place in all of Newfoundland and where the forest will burn is an experience few can ever enjoy. Yet, when the hunter or woodsman has been fortunate enough to set his tent at such a site, the *Mogazeesh*, *Obseet*, appears from the smoke to tell his story. Though you sit and listen until dawn's first ray before you sleep, you are refreshed beyond the good and power of sleep; indeed, refreshed for many days to follow and still, always and forever lighter in heart, for having heard the story of *Obseet*, the Red Indian boy

What language do you speak or hear? It matters little if you should listen to *Obseet*, for his is a language universal and all who hear it understand. Though he speaks the Beothuk tongue, foreign to you and to me, the words are clear to all within the circle of the flame.

Tonight, this very night, grey smoke rises beneath the starlit, moonlit sky on the shores of the silent water of a lake called *Shawayet*, a star. It has not been long since the first appearance of the fire and, though astonished, we do not try and stifle the flame, for we recognize this as no menace. It does, in fact, emit a feeling of peace and warmth. The smoke, regardless of shifting drafts about the camp, floats straight upward toward the stars and the moon, so our eyes remain forever clear.

As we watch, sitting quietly before our evening tent, the boy *Obseet* steps lightly from the smoke above the flame.

"Welcome, my friends, welcome to my home. My name is *Obseet*. *Obseet* means little bird in your tongue, and I was named so because I am so fleet. I can run so fast that as a man I once caught a fat stag on foot and, bringing him to the ground, I killed him with my knife. But I was named long before that time.

"Do you know where I came from? It was from out of the ground. Out of the ground from the centre of a triangle made by three arrows with white feather shafts right on the floor of our *mammateek*, the home of my family. This is where we all came from though we were brought forth from the wombs of our mothers. To bring *Obseet* into the world, my father had first to set the arrows, and as a man I also did this so that my wife could bring forth our twins.

"In our *mammateek*, we were happy. Ours was a life of love and work. My father, mother, uncle, aunt and two cousins shared our home. We loved each other and worked together and with all our friends to hunt and trap and build, to live. Sometimes we stayed for many moons to the south or to the north or east or west. We travelled the rivers and lakes and forests together, never fearful, always together. Homage we paid to our Voice, for it was He who told us of the setting of the arrows, and He who made *Kuis*, our sun, to shine, and *Watshoosooch*, the rain, to fall and He who guided all our living and, indeed, each of our lives.

"We slept in winter curled before our *mammateek* fire, *Boobeeshawt*, and we slept in summer in this same place though there was no flame. We boiled our meat and fish in birch rind and we ate our berries also from containers of birch. Our life was good. We had no enemy. All Beothuks were friends of one another and all animals were our friends too.

"I must tell you about our animals. The fish, the birds and the four legged creatures. As a boy I learned from my father and the other hunters of the tribe how to set the dead-fall for *Abidish*, the marten, and *Dogajavick*, the fox. With their skins, our mothers and sisters made clothes which we wrapped to our knees. The skin of Kosweet they used to tie and weave our furs into pieces that fit.

"*Kosweet* also served to make our *mammateek*. The hair was scraped from the leather to stretch over our poles and this was our home. We had many homes from the great water on all sides of our land to the centre of the forests at the long water Beothuk.

"On a day in September, all the tribe would gather at this, our central home, and plans were made for the great slaughter of our *Kosweet*. Men and boys worked to build storehouses and mend fences through which we drove the deer. The women spent much time sharpening the knives and making boxes for the meat. We boys would sharpen spears and points for arrows with the men for day upon day until the runner came to tell us of the movement of the deer. I myself because of my speed afoot, was a runner as a man and in October I was sent far to the south."

> *Obseet*, you are to journey as far as the open country south. When the deer become restless we must know. For there must be time to station the men beyond the fences to drive the deer. Our canoes and storehouses are ready. You will go and bring us word of the first movement.

"The leader of the hunt said to me, and I journeyed up the great tributary to the *Shebon* and into open country. There I saw thousands of deer. Great stags with their does vied for mastery and the supreme stags of all led their groups together. Once the deer were all together it would be but a matter of days before they began their journey, so with the first mated does I left for the fences and my people. Following the trails made centuries before by *Kosweet,* I found my people in two days' travel.

"The deer had begun to move, I told them. We must spread out from our fences into the country to encircle them.

"Our fences stretched along the river miles and miles from each of our storehouses and then into the country for three miles and more. From the ends of these wings into the forests and marshes we placed our men at intervals of calling distance. Fifty men we were who would walk with the deer to guide their movements into our great funnel, and at the river where the breaks in the fences were found were more than fifty men and all the women to kill our winter's food, give us shelter, our *moosins* and lace.

"We drove them, thousands strong, and in the water the spears and arrows found their marks until the *Shebon* became a channel of blood. And with us, far to the rear but coming into the fire light at night, was *Moisamadrook,* the wolf. *Moisamadrook* was our friend, for he killed the old and the sick among the herd of deer, but still we feared his presence because of his cries and cunning. To frighten *Moisamadrook* we would throw a birch rind torch at his gleaming eyes, and he would disappear into the night.

"We killed and cut and packed our meat. More work than this there was, for we must dress and scrape the hides. Nothing should be wasted, yet there was often too much killed for us to care for.

"We ate not only *Kosweet* but we slew *Mamshet* for food as well as clothing and *Guashawit,* the bear, whenever he came into our presence. With bone hook and thong line we caught *Wasemook,* the salmon, in spring and summer and on visits to the sea we took *Shamoth,* the caplin, and many other fishes. *Odensook* the goose, *Odjet,* the lobster, *Mamashet,* the duck and *Asson,* the gull, gave us much food too, and the eggs of many birds were sought during the months of spring.

"Yes, these animals and more were all our friends as were *Kuis, Adenishit,* the stars and the *Anoo-ee,* trees of the forest. Also our friends were the *Sho-ada-munk,* good humans from another land to the north with whom we traded and hunted.

"When I was sixteen I married *Emamooset,* a lovely pale girl, the finest worker of skins and furs in our tribe. With *modthamook,* the sinew of *Kosweet*, she could weave clothes of beauty, trimmed as no other woman could do.

"We were happy and content living in the home of her father and mother. Our life was quiet and full of love for all around us and regularly I placed the arrows so that if it willed the Voice, we should be given a child.

"One day a group of our men returned from a summer hunt far to the south and they brought wounded with them. Brought them home to die! Some had been killed in the south and left to be buried, should we find them later. My father was wounded and died in our *mammateek*. There were, he said, many *Sho-nocks*, people with whom we once hunted, trapped and lived for times, and they were armed with weapons of fire, for certain of *Asmudyin*, the Devil. We must now kill the *Sho-nock* if we were to live, he said.

"Now there was much sadness and women wailed. But many men prepared to return to bury our dead, and I with them, for my father had wished that I should go. We travelled six days to the valley where the *Sho-nocks* camped. By stealth we found our dead, now stinking and partly eaten by animals, their scalps removed and bodies naked. These we laid in shallow soil at night, covered with new skins we had brought for their burial. Not daring to meet the *Sho-nocks*, we returned to our home and our people.

"The struggle with the *Sho-nocks* signalled our end. Now we met with disasters in great numbers. For many generations we had occasionally seen the white man along the coast and fear of him sent us to the inside country for greater lengths of time, year on year. The *Sho-nock*, however, followed our country trails, destroyed our camps and stole our women.

"Now, too, our people began to suffer deaths from the cough and many were spitting blood among us. This, our elders said, was from the white fishermen along the coasts with whom we sometimes traded.

"We became accustomed to frequent death and sadness. Many people died and some were killed. We needed many to mend the fences and prepare our winter's larder, but we had no men to do the work.

"One day *Emamooset*, my beautiful wife, was wounded by a furrier who shot her as she bent cleaning fish on the banks of the *Shebon*. As she was complete with child, she died, but in death gave birth to my children, twin girls. Heavy with grief, I carried her body into the woodland, not far from here, to place her into a stone cave, wrapped in her own skins of *Mamshet*, trimmed about the neck and waist with soft furs of *Abidish*. There her bones remain for I covered the cave entrance with stone and no animal has destroyed the remnants of what once meant all of life to me.

"Now our people were few. We had to separate to live for we could not feed our numbers in the same manner as we had in the past with so few men to hunt. A meeting was held at our great house on the western shore of Beothuk's northern end. At that time many people elected to travel north and across the great deep water to the land of *Sho-ada-munk* the friendly people. But others did not wish to leave what they felt to be their last haven of safety and their home. As most of the elders were going to lead the tribal remnants north, I stayed with my mother, several other old women and a few babies. Two other young men also remained.

"Our winter alone was not an easy one. Indeed, we were beset by illness and fear such as we had never known. Our food supply was never large, and we three young men had always to hunt meat. We hunted down the stray, snow-caught deer, few that there were, and we cut open the house of *Mamshet* to kill the papoose. The small birds after which I was named were killed by any means we could and once we ate the flesh of *Abidish*.

"Two of the old women died in mid-winter and we carried them into the distant woods and left the bodies in as much shelter as we could make from three skins of *Kosweet*. Deep snows prevented us from taking proper care of our dead, though we hoped later to return and find a rock cave to place them in.

"Before spring a great storm came to the land. Our homes were almost buried in seven days of snow and we could not move, nor could any animal. For many weeks we lived on bark brew made from snow water and a few small birds. Only once or twice did we eat food we were accustomed to and, then, only the single partridge that flew into the opening by our *mammateek*.

"As soon as the snow settled enough for travelling we deemed it best to separate and make three paths to different settlements of white men and throw ourselves upon the mercy of those whom we first should meet. I took my mother and twin babies, who were then two years old, and set forth north-easterly for the sea water.

"After many days of slow and painful travel, made so from the weakness of hunger and the cold winter, we at last came within sighting distance of a settler's cabin. Standing on the cleared hill behind his home, I called and soon brought forth a man, armed with a weapon of fire. Unarmed and helpless, I shouted and waved my hands. The settler stood and watched and then raised his weapon to a shooting position. In vain I called, trying to communicate, and then in desperation I ran toward him, hoping somehow to show him I desired his friendship and help. For my life, I should not have done this, for he mistook my signs of supplication for hostility and when I was quite near he fired and killed me.

"One of my daughters was the last of our people to die. Her name was *Theeone*, meaning Heaven, and she lived with people such as you for twenty years. But she did not know of *Obseet* or any of her people, for she was too young to remember when all her Beothuk elders left her world. She knows us now.

"Listen, my friends! You or your people or the *Sho-nock* were not at fault. Had we understood one another our people would still travel the Indian Road, the free-living trail of expectation and hope. We are now, instead, united and my people are with your people and all people are brothers.

"My journey on Earth was short, by standards of earthly time, but my task is eternal. I was chosen from all our hunters from time everlasting to watch over the eternal spirit of the Red Indian Flame. This because I was the final Red Indian brave to perish from the earth and because I wished to speak to you and all who sit before me of my life and my task. I was happy to be chosen, though I see less of my people. As a man I worked, but as a youth I worked and played and also dreamed. It is as a youth that I was chosen as caretaker of the Beothuk flame. A youth with the wisdom of a man and knowledge of the life of all of my people. Youth portrays life, growth and hope. Endowed with much wisdom I stand before you now as *Mogazeesh*, a Red Indian boy.

"My people are no longer a part of your world, for we had no ability to communicate with you. Nor could you communicate with us. So, though we be together in one *mammateek*, we were far apart as the ends of the earth. Yet we are, in truth, one, and it is your task to learn this.

"Do not trouble yourselves to find the turning point between expendable life and death. Rather, think only in terms of love and truth, and these will justify all your acts for in love and truth lies the power to forgive. That power I give to you now. As my people have forgiven you, so you will now forgive all others.

"Now I must go. Where the flame will burn tomorrow I cannot tell, though I will be there. You have your legacy, that which was mine, the land and all the life thereon. Your destiny is to some day understand the harmony of the land and find the love that, though too often hidden, abounds throughout the world and its people."

The figure of the Red Indian boy faded into the curling smoke and the pungent smell of burning birch and fir tingled our nostrils, for the first time. Then the flame vanished. The night and all is gone, for over the *Annieopsquotch* hills the dawn is breaking.

Jim Barlow

There was a rumour around that someone had a moose snare up the river from Reidsville. The trail that led to the salmon pool was the access, it was said, and there were blazes across from the mouth of Crooked Feeder to where the snare was supposed to be. It was a cool day in late June, the wind was brisk from the southwest and the sun was shining. It was the cool air and the breeze that made me keep a jacket on.

A movement fifty yards ahead at a bend in the trail caused me to stop. It was surely a man that I'd seen part of, stepping off the trail. I walked slowly ahead and when I was a few feet from where I had placed the movement, I stopped and examined the thin trunks of fir and spruce off the trail, and there he was. Just a little of the back of his worn mackinaw showed, motionless, from behind the largest trunk about ten feet from the trail.

"What are you doing in there?" I asked.

There was no movement and no response. I waited for a moment and took a couple of steps off the trail toward him, looking carefully behind the trees, and the man came from around the tree trunk and strolled slowly out to the path.

"Thought I might have left some slips out," he said, "and I didn't want to break the law." He knew who I was.

He was a little man and his torn and worn clothing hung too large and baggy over his bony frame. He hadn't shaved for days or maybe weeks and tobacco stain seeped from the lips that mostly hid his toothless gums.

"Wait here a second," I told him, and I began to look around all the trees near where he had stood. From behind one I picked up a Cooey single-shot .22. Back on the trail I asked, "Is this yours?"

Poor fellow, what was he to say? "Yes" and he'd probably lose it. "No" and it probably meant going to court and losing the rifle anyway.

"Yep," he said.

We talked awhile and he accompanied me as I searched for the moose snare which he said he didn't know about. The blazes were there though and someone had once had a snare on a moose trail through the alder bed. It was gone now. There was no telephone wire around. Still, you could see where the wire had been tied to a leaning fir angled across the trail.

I seized his rifle and asked the local RCMP to return it to him in a couple of weeks. To have charged him and taken up time before a magistrate would have gained little. If fined, the money would have been moved from Welfare to Natural Resources, a matter of bookkeeping. It was better to keep him in suspense, worrying about what could happen and then have him disturbed by a visit from the Mounties. I told him what could happen but let him wait and wonder and worry. His rifle meant a great deal to him.

Like Jim Barlow, this fellow was a part of Newfoundland's unemployed in the 50s. There has always been "unemployment" in Newfoundland. That is to say, there were always times when men were idle even from sealing or fishing, hunting or trapping or cutting pulp. After Confederation, however, things began to change so that many who were necessarily idle for a part of the year, and had always been, were now paid for a part of those idle times. For the most part the recipients changed their lives but little when this happened, but for some, the little incentive to work they might once have had was gone.

❧

Jim Barlow sat crosswise in the doorway of his wallboard shack, his back against the casing. Occasionally he moved his head a trifle, crooked his neck and squinted toward the other shore. His shack by the river had a metal roof and the sun reflected from it, making it hard for Jim to see. The corner of the shack was right in line with the fields he was watching across the river.

Among the possible solutions to the problem was to move either behind the shack or out in front of it, where the fence used to be. Neither solution would be practical from Jim's point of view, however, for both would move him from the shade of his own doorway, the only shade anywhere around the dwelling, and both would also force him to place his jug right out in the hot sun. He could, of course, leave the jug and move only himself, but that obviously wouldn't do since he'd then have to keep moving back and forth from the hot sun to the jug and back—and so on.

The heat was oppressive. There was no breeze, a fact attested to by the placid water of the Humber River which today drifted smooth and lazy-like through the middle of Dunnsville. Sometimes, in the spring of the year, ice rushed by the shacks, littering the riverbank, crunching and grinding its noisy way to the sea. In the fall heavy rains made the river a menace to these same shacks, now so safely above the waterline. It was early August, low water time, and the river appeared motionless, slow-moving like the day and the folks that lived alongside, like Jim.

Jim reached around the door casing for his jug, hooked the handle with his thumb and cradled it neatly to his thin lips. The cool liquid dripped down his chin and a quiver in his lower lip let a little stream trickle away from his toothless gums onto his tattered shirt.

"Blood of a bitch," Jim swore, as the juice dribbled down and he let the jug down with a thud. But then, as the liquid soaked through the thin shirt, cooling his skinny chest, a smile cut the hollow cheeks away from his mouth. The wetting actually felt good and for a moment he toyed with the idea of pouring the entire contents over him just to cool off. But the idea soon clouded over and Jim wheezed a short, downward sigh, closed his eyes and leaned back against the door jamb once again.

A groan from inside the cabin stirred him. Jim opened his eyes, cocked his head and listened. The groan came again, this time with a "Jim" falling heavily at the end. Jim worked himself to his feet and ambled unsteadily into the bedroom where his wife Maude lay on the worn mattress of an iron bed. She was sweating. Her ponderous breasts dropped down from the curve of her chest on either side and her swollen belly heaved with her laboured breathing.

"It's comin', Jim, git the doctor," she whispered.

Jim leaned over the foot of the bed, staring. After a minute or two he moved backward, staggering slightly. "Foot's asleep," he said.

Maude Barlow was naked, all two hundred pounds of her. She was a short, heavy woman with stern features and stringy hair, now wet with sweat. She had born eleven children, ten girls and a son. Jim moved toward the side of the bed and dropped his skinny butt on the edge of the dirty sheet that partly covered the mattress.

"Shore wish Kitty would come home," he said. "Is she comin'?"

His wife nodded but didn't speak. Her stern mouth was clenched from discomfort and anger and she turned on her side, bringing her knees up toward the weight as she moved.

"Kitty ain't been home since she got married. Shore will be good to have her around agin," Jim mumbled.

"You git to hell out and git the doctor, damn you!"

Jim jumped up at this sudden outbreak. He'd thought his wife too sick to sound off like that. Hell, she musn't be sick. He looked at her a moment before making up his mind. Maude's staring face would have been enough but when she said "Git!" Jim moved.

He ambled, a little shakily, outside into the sun and headed for Mrs. Wood's house next to the bridge. As he passed the line of wooden stubs where his fence used to be, he glanced across the river. What he saw made him draw up shortly. It was them damned sheep belongin' to that son-of-a-bitch Nelson and they were right in line with the tin roof of his shack, only now that he was out along the old fence line he could see the other side of the river clearly. There was no glare.

"Them god-damned sheep were probably there all the time," he muttered half aloud. "Shit!"

Jim sat down on one of the fence stumps which stood in a line along the boundary of the land Jim had claimed when he first squatted. The fence, about sixty feet from the house, had been here when Jim got the property ten years ago. Each winter had taken its toll, however, for juniper sticks make a wonderful hot fire and the temptation to cut a couple occasionally, in place of travelling further to get dry wood, was too powerful to resist. Now only a small square of little round stumps marked his land. They stood maybe a foot from ground level and were visible all the time except during winter because no grass grew on the barren, sandy foot-trampled yard.

Sitting on one of these stubs now was really fairly tricky. It wasn't comfortable, and in order to balance himself, Jim had to draw his bony knees up and hold them with both arms. He heard the babbles and crys of some of his children as he sat here thinking, but he paid no heed to them when they came up beside him. They crowded about him, partly blocking his view across the river, trying and see what Jim saw. One, a tiny, flat-nosed blond girl, was crying, blood streaming from her mouth. Two other blond look-alike sisters, one slightly larger than the other, tried to comfort her with appeals of assurance as they petted and hugged her.

"Six of them," Jim said aloud.

"Six what?" one girl asked.

"Six sheep," said the bigger girl and laughed.

She laughed harder and hollered, "Six of us too, six of us too," as more of them took up the chant, so that soon they were all jabbering, some not so clearly since they were very young. "Six of us too, six of us too." It was changed to "sick" and "sit" and "sip" and, finally, inevitably, "shit."

"Shit of us too, shit of us too." The girls tugged at one another, shouting and laughing until, in a rush, the dirty bigger girl, the oldest, pushed Jim and he lost his balance from the fence post butt.

Screeching and laughing, the girl, Lucy, fell over him, followed by the others, even to the tiniest, now with blood dried and caked to her nose and lips. Jim tried desperately to shove them off, swearing and yelping like a dog with its tail caught in a door. Lucy, who was twelve now, was tenacious and strong and it was not easy to shove her off. She clung desperately to him, laughing and calling "shit of us, shit of us." Jim grabbed her hands finally and ripped them from his waist, breaking loose as he did so. His shirt had been ripped more and the one remaining button holding his fly together had parted company from the cloth.

He stood apart now and pointed his finger at the laughing demons. Lucy lay on the ground, her dress flapping about her waist, sobbing with uncontrolled laughter.

"God damn! You git over to Mrs. Woods quick and tell her Ma wants her now and tell her to fetch the doctor!"

Ginny, a ten-year-old, turned and ran quickly, followed by Lucy and two of the others. The smallest children, blood-caked Jo and five-year-old Cathy, stopped laughing now. Their hollering ceased as they watched their sisters running away toward the bridge.

Jim turned and went back to the shack door. Quietly he reached around the frame and picked up with one hand the rifle he had been holding most of the day. He lifted the jug with the other. He walked around behind the shack and down over the bank to the river.

By nine o'clock it was just getting duckish. Jim had long ago fired all the shells he had and had consumed what remained in his jug. Now he was sleeping. His bed was a sand bank, sloping gently upward from the water of the river. From that vantage point he had been able to see all the sheep and had fired at most of them at least once, although it was hard to tell whether he had actually hit any or not. Unless they were hit in the head or the heart they usually just trembled a little when they were hit with a .22 bullet. At times they moved away slowly and sometimes they ran. You could hardly see a tremble from where Jim lay.

"Hey, Pop!"

Jim almost heard it in his half-sleep. He rolled over and stretched. The rifle had dropped into the sand, nose down.

"Pop! Where the Jesus are ya?" came the call again.

Jim jerked his head up. "That Kitty?" he asked himself, wonderingly.

Being half asleep he wasn't sure, although he would know her voice anywhere, asleep or not. It sounded like Ann, though he didn't like Ann. She was always snooty somehow. He really wanted it to be Kitty, so he thought maybe it was.

He got up, yawned, bent over, picked the rifle up out of the sand and walked up and over the bank. At the crest of the slope he tripped and fell flat on his stomach. Ann was watching from the doorway and she laughed.

Jim lay there seething. He had a good mind not to get up. "God damn her," he grunted.

"Pop, come on in and see your new baby daughter," the girl shouted. Her suppressed laughter made her voice quake just a little and she broke into hysteria again after she'd shouted.

Jim watched her turn and disappear into the shack. After she'd gone, he got up. Tilting sideways occasionally, he made his way to the door.

Inside the bedroom it was stuffy. Life and the odors of life and dirt filled the space. A kerosene lamp had been lit and placed on the table in the corner. This was always necessary in the evening because there were no windows.

Mrs. Wood was there. Jim could see that. She was a big woman, weighing well over 250 pounds. You could hardly miss her. Nobody could. Ann and most of the children, at least all that were still home, were in the room. Mrs. Wood had left the last baby, the one with no name yet, at her place. She had been keeping her for the past few days and that's where she was now, at Woods' house, out of the way.

"What do ya think of the baby, Pop?" The voice came from another older girl, blond, with broad hips and heavy breasts. She wore a man's shirt open two buttons down, and expertly rolled a cigarette from makings as she stood at the door of the girls' bedroom. It was dark where she was and Jim hadn't seen her until she spoke.

Mrs. Wood moved away from the bed a bit so Jim could see the tiny, red creature lying peacefully beside the fat mountain that was its mother. Jim's eyes glistened as he looked past the newborn toward Kitty in the dark doorway. "By God, Kitty, it's shore good to see ya," he said.

About nine o'clock the next morning an RCMP car was in the yard, which was nothing new either to Jim or to the neighbours. Members of the local detachment spent an inordinately large portion of their time in Dunnsville, especially close along the river's east bank. People in this area, people like Jim, had a way of drawing attention to themselves with sporadic family disputes, the presence of fresh moose meat in March month, the selling of quart bottles of Jockey Club, occasional puncheons of home brew and, in this case, a complaint from the brothers Nelson that several panes of glass had been mysteriously shattered in their barn and that several small bullet holes had suddenly appeared in both the side of their barn and the sides of their outhouse. Bullet holes in a barn that had no living creature, save two cats and perhaps a rat or two, was of relatively little consequence, but bullet holes in an outhouse were quite another thing. There were no bullet holes discovered any place else, incidentally, none in sheep, for instance. The source of the fusillade was not known but it was certainly from across the river and apparently from the direction of Jim's house.

Cpl. Grogan was well known by everyone in Dunnsville and everyone there was certainly well known to Cpl. Grogan. In fact, Grogan may have been the most frequent unrelated visitor to the Barlow homestead, probably making him the central figure in Jim's outside social life. The Corporal's first visit was ten years ago, soon after the Barlows with their then small flock of blond progeny had moved in. During one of their frequent connubial disagreements Maude had chosen to smash her disagreeable little mate in the face with a very hot cast iron skillet. This aggressive spousal behaviour had so enraged Jim that the neighbours for quite some distance away had flooded the local detachment office with phone calls, announcing probable murder and certain mayhem, deduced from Jim's howls of rage and pain and Maude's equally loud bellows of threat and defiance. Today's visit was only cursory, however. No need to get involved in the domestic issue of the day, whatever it might be. There was only need to ask a few questions and look around for shell cases maybe. But there were no shell casings since two of the smaller children had collected them and hidden their treasure in a secret cache, never to be found by anyone save themselves, like so much pirate gold in buried chests and money pits all around the Island. Jim had no inkling of how such a thing could have occurred across the river at the brothers Nelson. But he did wonder about the sheep and came very close to asking Grogan how many of Nelson's sheep were dead or wounded. It is one of the great wonders of this or any other age that Jim had the wit to hold his tongue, this one time.

After Grogan left Jim assumed his regular post in the doorway. His many younger offspring shouted and cried their usual cacophony. Kitty and Ann busied themselves looking after Maude and the newest Barlow, and Mrs. Wood, next door, kept the yearling Barlow sprout tied with a short string to her back step. Jim, however, was deeply concerned. He had fired all of his .22 shells and either consumed or spilled the very last drop from his jug.

"What the God-damned buggering hell," he mumbled as he jammed his hands into both pockets of his torn pants, hoping to find a coin or two. But instead, his hands reached straight through to his genitals, which he now began to explore carefully. Maude had long since ceased to repair the holes in Jim's clothes, barely having the time to keep dresses or some reasonable facsimile on her girl flock and trousers on the fourteen-year-old boy.

It would be a week before Jim could cash another welfare check. He leaned back against the door jamb, muttering profanities and gradually smiling a little as he began to enjoy the holes in his pockets.

Excerpts From Pearl's Letters Home

Dear Folks

May, 1955

Imagine! It's only ten o'clock in the morning Newfoundland time (eight-thirty your time) and I'm up at the cold office typing this letter. The sun was shining so beautifully when I woke up that I thought I would dash thru these letters and then go home to clean out the cellar. But the sun isn't shining any more and the clouds are threatening.

There she is, the little imp! That Sheila Hall just loves to dilly dally on her way to school. Since she's supposed to be there at nine-thirty she's a wee bit late. She's skipping rope, if you can imagine skipping rope on a muddy, rutty road. Now she's stopped in front of our house pretending to do something, just wishing someone would come out and holler "hi." There will be no scolding by the teacher, she doesn't care that much. Sheila is so nonchalant about it all—life is just a breeze. She's really a very intelligent and delightful girl and it's a shame the school can't offer the kids better training.

Last night Sheila and a couple of her girlfriends stopped in the house on the way from school. They had just completed sweeping their schoolroom, a chore all the children take turns at every second night. Saves on janitors.

The school is a three-room affair, round pot belly stove in each room and kerosene lamps on the walls. There are eighty—ninety pupils through grade nine. However, they do teach through grade eleven. Five years ago they had one room, so really the school is growing and improving.

A couple of days ago Sheila's five-year-old brother, Stevie, looked out the window and hollered, "The Mounties are coming! The Mounties are coming!" and flew under the bed, scared to pieces. His mother looked out the window and there was Sheila strutting down the road with an American soldier (from Harmon Air Force Base) on each side, talking a mile a minute. They were looking for Steve so he could issue them a gun permit and Sheila was showing them the way, proud as punch. Poor Stevie.

June, 1955

Got a new toilet seat put in today. Hallelujah! Oh, we've always had a toilet, mind you, but when the house was left empty last winter, water left in the bowl froze and cracked. I've been forever wiping up the floor. Some days the odour is a bit offensive. The flush box needs a certain kind of screw, though, 'cause if the plunger isn't properly seated the water keeps running and pretty soon all that pumped-by-hand-water is gone.

July, 1955

The big news in Cormack is the stealing of the safe from the Cormack Co-op Society. This is our store. I say 'our' because it is owned by the Cormack residents. Cormack folk have the privilege of buying shares and the profits are divided among the stockholders annually. This store realizes a sizeable profit, only right now all assets are frozen, paying for the electric wiring of the store and the meat freezer. The Dodds own *one* share—we hope to buy more.

Although *only* two thousand dollars cash was in the safe all the records were there too. The records contained all the names of folks owing money to the store, which amounted to around six thousand dollars. So some folks stand to gain by this robbery. We found it more interesting because the Mounties took Art Taylor (store manager), Don, Steve and Selby into their confidence, telling them who the suspects were, the description of their car and license number, and asked them to report any findings. The fellas had a lot of fun deciding what their next move would be if they were the robbers and Don made trips into the byroads looking for tire marks. Don didn't check the one road that he felt just wouldn't be the one because it was too near a public campground but, wouldn't you know, this was the road the Mounties discovered the safe on!

Tuesday night he accompanied the Mounties to this spot to help carry the safe out and search for the ledgers and records, which were buried under the moss. Four men are behind bars and a fifth has skipped town. Two thousand dollars divided between five men is hardly worth the bother of stealing a six hundred pound safe.

August, 1955

Sheila was recently confirmed and this is a big event in the life of a Roman Catholic girl. Her Aunt Jean and young Stevie went with her. Jean took several pictures of Sheila and the priest and one of Sheila kissing the Bishop's ring. After the kiss, apparently the Bishop left his hand extended and Stevie went up to it. On the way home after the ceremony, as they were discussing the happy event, Sheila boasted of kissing the Bishop's ring. Stevie, full of innocence, said, "I smelled it. I though you were supposed to smell it!"

January, 1956

There are two letters from Don's mother and two letters from my mom that are in need of answering, and I wanted to drop Gram and Rip a line, so thought I'd solve all this by writing a general letter. I seem to be slipping when it comes to answering letters lately. It just seems that there is nothing new to write about and I can't seem to find the time. Each day is like the day before.

The most talked about subject is the weather. It has been 29 degrees below, winds and five feet of snow. It's been hard on our kerosene bill and the wood pile. We've been able to keep warm with our new space heater and that's a blessing. Many families here in Cormack use the living room as a bedroom (so many children) and the kitchen is their only source of heat. One family was telling how they stoked up the kitchen fire on going to bed until they discovered the chimney was cracked. Now they don't dare leave a fire in it all night. The mother got up during the night to check the children and found their blankets frozen to the wall!

There were enough carrots, beets and potatoes in the cellar to last until spring, but they all froze. Canned carrots in the pantry froze. Enough about this cold weather and we've had quite enough of it too!

February, 1956

The last two weeks have been a nightmare and we're just now getting out from under the stress. Never before has so tragic an event been so close to us.

Monday, January 30, Margaret Hall (our closest neighbour and Steve's wife) was ill so I asked the children, Sheila and Stevie, to stay with us. The doctor was down Sunday night and said Margaret's illness was due to nerves mostly and to pay little attention to it, so we didn't. Monday I saw her, washed her face and hands, helped her brush her teeth and talked to her. Tuesday she wasn't better, but the doctor had sent some sleeping pills which would give her the needed rest. I talked with her that day, but she couldn't talk very well. Her hands were cold and I rubbed them. Still, no one thought her very ill. We didn't know. No one did.

Tuesday night Margaret died. We couldn't believe it when Heber pounded at the door in the night and said Steve thought Margaret was dead but he wasn't sure. What an ungodly place out here to be ill! No phone, fourteen miles to a doctor. We still can't believe it and every day we re-live the tragedy. It was a stroke or a series of strokes but no one knew how ill she was. Certainly not the doctor! Margaret was only thirty-seven.

From then on there were sleepless nights, with Don and Art taking care of arrangements from getting the priest to buying the casket handles. We now realize what wonderful people live here. Folks who hardly knew the Halls turned out to help, to do anything possible.

The most difficult chore was Steve's—telling the children. He told them the truth and was completely honest with them. It breaks my heart to think of these two little kids without a mother. Stevie is six and is not too greatly affected, as of now. Sheila, at nine, has become quite sensitive and expects a great deal of her father's attention, whereas he has always been strict and rather distant with them. But I believe with love and proper discipline all can turn out well.

They all are living with us now, with Steve in one spare bedroom and the children in the other spare room. They each have a bed and dresser and their clothes and toys are here. Our home is their home until something better can be worked out. Steve hopes he can persuade his widowed sister and small child to leave Toronto and come to Cormack to make a home for them. I wonder if she will?

Steve left Monday with the children for a week with his mother and aged grandmother. I have spent the week cleaning house. Never has my home been dirtier, but never has it mattered less. During that week there were people and dirty boots all over the house. At meal time there were anywhere from two to nine at the table. They will be back with us again Monday the 13th (Sheila's birthday) and we'll get on schedule. Now you see why there hasn't been the time, energy or desire to write letters home.

April, 1956

The little adoption announcement tells the story! I'll try not to devote this whole letter to little Tracy Donald, but having acquired quite a bit of maternal and paternal pride, we find that a good many of our waking hours and many of our should-be-sleeping hours are spent thinking about and caring for him. He's a real sweetheart.

Tracy was born April 11, 12:10 a.m. (two days before my birthday), weighing nine and a half pounds. He arrived at our home on Thursday, April 19, after a two-hour ride from Corner Brook, over such muddy, rutty roads that Don had to kick the truck into low as we scraped through the mess. At times we were afraid we wouldn't make it. We have already taken him into Dr. Byrne in Deer Lake for a check-up to assure us all is okay. We know so little about and caring for babies. The best read book in the house is Dr. Spock's *Baby and Child Care*—indispensable.

September, 1956

What Don and I talked about even before we arrived here and what many in Cormack talk about once in a while finally came about. Folks would say, "Let's do something...," "It's a problem, but...," etc. etc. There is quite a crop of teenagers here in Cormack with nothing to do and no place to go. Occasionally they get to a movie in Deer Lake, but their school is their only activity. Some of the kids spend their evenings walking up and down the road. That's it.

Last Friday we had our first Teenager's Club meeting. We were thrilled to have sixteen young folks at our home. They seemed equally as thrilled to come. There was an evening's entertainment of group games, card playing, discussion and refreshments. They're a good group of kids, and co-operative. We have a winter's plan of cards, sleigh rides, song fests, skating parties, hikes and dancing, and hope to get together every other week. Friday the 14th will be our Halloween party, a bit early I know. One of our spare rooms is being converted into a 'ghost room' and there will be bobbing for apples, eating fried cakes and marshmallows on a string and, of course, we will all be in costume.

Our aim is to get use of a warehouse to be used as a community hall. If this comes about we can accommodate a bigger group, have a ping pong table and hold dances. What we need most is co-operation from the parents and the community. We would like so much to have this Teenager's Club grow into a strong and permanent part of Cormack.

November, 1956

The Teenager's Halloween Party was a howling success, with nineteen young folks here. Plus we had a friend in as a week-end guest. Twenty-two meant darn near a houseful. There were the usual Halloween activities—bobbing for apples, eating fried cakes on a string (first fried cakes I'd ever made), couples chewing string to a marshmallow in the middle and pushing a potato across the room with the nose. Frankly, I'd never tried these games and if you think they're easy, try them. They are not, but are a great deal of fun. What stole the show was our Ghost House. It wasn't that there were so many props in the Ghost House, but Don took each person thru and it was his gift of gab that made it a thriller. You see, he would say he found a dead man that afternoon and brought him home. Why, you could feel his hair (moose hair), and his face (a stuffed rubber glove) was still warm! Of course, the corpse had to be dissected and here was his liver (real liver) and innards (cooked spaghetti). They walked a plank and crawled through a barrel. The room was dark and the kids were blindfolded. Some were so frightened Don had to bring them out of the room before he was thru with his ghost story. A prize was given for the best costume—an old shoe wrapped up in newspaper.

The folks were appreciative, but the next morning when I had to mop up the mud I felt like a dishrag and wondered if it was worth it. There have been so many interested youth that the decision was reached that no more could come—there just isn't enough room. Four kids came that night and wanted to join. I'd never seen them before and had to send them away. The next meeting will be a quiet one—cards, checkers, dominoes, Chinese checkers, scrabble—and they must take their shoes off!

February, 1957

It was a year ago Thursday night that Margaret Hall passed away. Since then the children have had a variety of homes, from living with us to Mrs. O'Quinn as a housekeeper. She left recently and Steve was glad. He kept house by himself for a few weeks. Recently a cousin from Bonne Bay came to keep house. Her husband works in the woods in the winters and she and their fifteen-year-old son and an elderly boarder lived alone. Her son and the boarder came with her. There is a houseful at Hall's, but she is a fine housekeeper and good cook and the children are crazy about her. The first time Don met her she was plainly dressed, a rather simple looking woman. Next time he saw her he did not know her. She had lipstick and rouge on, strong perfume, two-tone glasses and a cigarette in her mouth.

May, 1957

By now you have received our announcement of the arrival of our adopted little girl, Kathleen Susan. You must think us terribly courageous or terribly crazy. Sometimes we wonder too. However, Kathy is such a lovely baby we couldn't resist her. She suits us perfectly. Let me tell you a bit about her. Born March 1, weight 8 pounds, 5 ounces. She has fair complexion, pretty blue eyes, and what hair she has is rather auburn. She's an extremely bright child, very happy, talks and smiles a great deal. She's easy to care for, if only because I don't have time to fuss over her. One difficulty, however, is that she 'ups' frequently during each bottle, but the doctor says she will outgrow this. We love her dearly.

July, 1957

A rather unique wedding takes place this evening at the school. The older girl is from Deer Lake and has been living with a man here in Cormack. She is well known as, well, to put it mildly, a very disreputable girl. She is very young and she brought in her fifteen-year-old sister to live the same life. Now this little sister is getting married. The boy she's marrying seems quite nice and comes from a very strict Salvation Army family. It's believed his father is forcing the marriage.

It will probably be a rowdy affair (imagine, in a school!), but being very close to the school we thought we'd drop in just for the heck of it. But, I'll be darned if the two sisters didn't come to the house this morning and personally invite us to the wedding. And we'll go!

The older sister did all the talking and the young bride-to-be, eight months pregnant, looked on with a sort of silly, scared-to-death look. The older girl remarked she wouldn't guarantee there would be a wedding because the bride-to-be was sick yesterday and wasn't feeling any too well today. She sure hoped nothing would happen as she was looking forward to the dance afterwards!

July, 1958

There has been quite a crop of babies in Cormack lately. Young Mary, age about seven, called out to Mrs. Hillier (our local nurse or midwife) one day and said, "Mrs. Hillier, you know what?" "No, what, Mary," asked Mrs. Hillier. "The old lady's going to have another baby." She's the same girl who last year, when her mother had boy number five, said, "Another f___ boy!" She's what is known as a hard case.

Eric and Eileen Johnston and their two adopted children, ages three years and five months, are coming next Tuesday for the day and for some fishing. It'll be a bit like a nursery here and I'm looking forward to it. He's manager of the Glynmill Inn in Corner Brook and I know they'll come loaded with many goodies. We first got acquainted with them when Don picked him and his buddy up with well over their limit of trout last year. Eileen tells her story of being up with their baby most of one night. One of the early morning cleaning women arrived and inquired how the baby was. Eileen, in bathrobe, pincurls, a bit rumpled and tired, said, "Just fine." The cleaning woman replied, "Well, my dear, it sure shows on you!"

Love,
Pearl

A Long Night In Codroy

A loose board beneath the roof overhang just outside the little bedroom banged at intervals as the wind lifted it and then allowed it to drop with each waning gust. I was snugly sunken in the feather mattress of my bed listening to this occasional clatter when sleep gradually overtook me. Then, in my sleep, this banging of the loose board became a knock.

The knocking was hard and insistent when I awoke in the rather uncomfortable daybed set in the living room of our Cormack house. We had been sleeping on the daybed, Pearl and I, since Stevie and Sheila had come to stay with us for a few days while their mother recovered from an illness diagnosed by the doctor as hysteria, an artifact, he said, of menopause.

I crawled out and shuffled over a cold linoleum floor through the kitchen to the back door, the only accessible one this winter since ten feet of drifted snow almost obscured the front entrance. The pounding was continuous until I clicked the latch and pulled the door open to face an excited Heber Roberts.

"Don boy, you gotta come," he said, "I think Margaret is dead!"

Shocked speechless, it was a full minute before I could recover. "She can't be. My God, Heber, it's not possible."

"I think she is, boy, hurry up and come and see," he said. "I'll get on back to Steve."

I closed the door on the good-hearted neighbour and rushed back to our living room. There Pearl was sitting up watching me and now anxiously asked what had happened.

"Heber said he thinks Margaret is dead," I said as I began to dress; long-johns first, trousers, socks and shirts and several sweaters. "He's gone back to be with Steve."

Pearl's reaction was the same as mine; incredulous, shocked and disbelieving. "Dead," she whispered, for fear the kids would hear. "Oh, God, what about the children?"

It was a sub-zero midnight in February. Snow covered the ground with alternating layers of frozen crusts and granular pellets topped by several inches of light fluff and the wind was blowing, drifting the new, light surface snow across the by-roads. Rather than try and move the truck into the road from the outside gate, I walked the thousand feet following Heber's tracks, already partly obscured, to Steve's house.

Margaret lay on her back in her bed with the covers neatly laid across her body under her chin. It looked to me as though she had been lying this quietly for hours. Her arms were outside the bedspread, resting with the fingers of her hands barely touching across her pelvic area and her eyes were closed.

Steve sat at the foot of the bed. He was nervous and distraught and I could see that his eyes were bloodshot as he looked up at me. "Is she dead?" he asked.

I put my hand on his wife's forehead and it was cold. I picked up her right wrist and felt for a pulse. Then I tried for a pulse in her left one. There was no pulse in either cold and slightly stiffened wrist or in her neck as I felt.

"Have you got a mirror?"

"There's one on the dresser, over there," Steve said, pointing. Heber, who'd been standing by Steve's chair with his hands resting on his friend's shoulders, stepped over and handed it to me. I held it in front of Margaret's face a moment, turned it, looked at it and then rubbed my finger across the glass. There was no sign of a breath; no moisture. Finally, I bent and listened, put my ear next to her nose and then dropped my head over her heart. Nothing, no sound, no movement and no life. Her cold skin suggested to me that she had indeed been dead for hours. I went over to Steve and told him that I thought, yes, she was dead.

Steve broke into sobs with his head in his hands. "What am I going to do? There's no priest and it's probably too late. I bathed her this afternoon and she only just mumbled to me. I had to pick her up out of the tub and carry her to bed. I thought it was just the medicine." Then he broke, sobbed loudly, tears rolling down his slender face.

"Heber," I said, holding my keys out toward him. "See if you can dig my truck out and get to Art Taylor's. Ask him to fetch the Monsignor and Dr. O'Quinn as quickly as he can. The priest, for sure, but get them both."

I stayed in the bedroom with Steve and his dead Margaret, listening to the sorrow and trying to console, for a long time it seemed, until Heber returned and got a pot of tea on the kitchen stove. Then, leaving Steve to be alone with the woman he'd married in England during the war, as he asked to be now, I went into the kitchen.

"I stopped and told Pearl," Heber said. "I thought she might be worried."

We drank tea and talked of nothing. It was all so unreal. Finally, we heard voices coming from outside. Coming, it seemed to me then, from another world.

It was after 2:00 a.m. and Art had returned with Monsignor Doyle. He had also found Dr. O'Quinn, but the doctor, who had been playing cards with the weekly poker crew, was coming in his own car. Art said that the roads were real bad and the by-road was filling in fast. He mightn't even be able to turn around, he thought.

Dr. O'Quinn was drunk when he arrived and so was Peter, the fire chief, who accompanied him. They came into the kitchen shouting over each other's recklessness behind the wheel. O'Quinn, who had difficulty standing without placing his feet fairly wide apart, was contemptuous of Peter who had apparently started out driving only to loose control to O'Quinn.

"Undependable in an emergency," O'Quinn slurred, pointing at Peter, who had dropped heavily onto a kitchen chair. "Undependable, unconscionably undependable in a time of crisis," he said, wagging a wavering finger at the tip of his unsteady arm. "Shame, shame, Peter. It's a good thing I took over or we'd be in a snowbank; probably dead. God, my God, what a fire chief! No damned good as a recruit for the cause, Peter. We'd never be able to trust a drunk when we start blowing up those limey bastards again." An ardent IRA politicist, O'Quinn vowed each time he became drunk, which seemed to many to be most of the time, that his outlawed army would one day rise again and crush the English invaders.

The doctor was a big man whose disease at times made him a worry. Oh yes, a worry indeed, for witness poor Margaret's death.

A year after this sad occasion O'Quinn left with his wife. Soon after his departure, jaundiced and on his back with what was believed almost total liver failure, his death was reported (mistakenly, it turned out) in a rather flattering obituary drafted by the Newfoundland correspondent of a Commonwealth medical journal. We heard afterward that the good doctor had taken the cure and was well enough for several years to accomplish near miracles patching holes in IRA militants whose bombs had either exploded too quickly or who had become successful targets of Protestant aggressors or British "occupation" troops.

At the time of his departure a local cramp hand had wagged that for the first time in three years our old O'Quinn was flat on his back while his wife was on her feet attending him. "A shocking change," he said.

Leaving the priest and the doctor to sort out the compassionate, the theological and biological implications of death and times of death, last rites and the peace of Margaret's soul with her grieving husband, Heber, Art and I left to fetch Mrs. White, the kindly midwife of our community, who also washed, dressed and laid out the dead. Heber had searched about and located some biscuits which we left on the kitchen table to accompany the tea to refresh the bereaved and broken husband, the representatives of the church and the medical profession and the sobering Peter.

The road was passable, but only for a few yards at a stretch. Backing up, again and again, we changed into low and slammed through drifts, getting hung up only once that required our shovelling and pushing as we spun and roared west, slewed around the corner and down the rear by-road to the White house, a full two miles. While Art and I managed with much shovelling (and more luck) to get the half-ton Fargo, with its load of birch sticks and snow, turned around, Heber plowed crotch deep in snow to the back door and pounded, as he had earlier in that dark, stormy night, on mine.

It wasn't easy for Mrs. White to make it to the Fargo, but with Heber's considerable strength, his arms about her hefty body, they made it together and soon she was safely ensconced in the hall kitchen and fully in charge of the food, the men, the sorrow and all that had to be done. It had been a full cab with the four of us, but the added weight must surely have helped.

The remainder of the night was less trying for all hands now. The priest, doctor and fire chief returned to their homes and made it safely. Heber and Art went to their homes and Steve accompanied me to our house for a fitful, waking hour or two, 'till dawn broke. Then he woke his children, Sheila and Stevie, and told them.

It was past nine in the morning when Art and I arrived at the rectory for Steve, following his wishes, as he felt them at the time. Heber and Mrs. White took the responsibility of getting the pine boards for our cabinet maker neighbour to make the coffin, as well as satin and cotton and tacks and things for the women to gussy up the inside of the box.

The morning was bright and cold at 15 degrees below (Fahrenheit), the wind was brisk, but had slacked a bit and the scads of snow, of course, had left off. We were greeted by the housekeeper, who led us to the study after we'd shed our boots and called out our arrival to the Monsignor.

"Come in, come in. Take a spell," he said, smiling at us from his plush chair by a crackling fire in the fireplace. "You fellas must be tired the way you turned to last night. It was all ree-raw last night, but it's all straightened up now, isn't it boys?" Then he called to his housekeeper. "Mrs. Rowsell, give us a drop of rum in that tea you're fixin'."

An hour with the priest sped by quickly and we'd had three well-laced cups of tea before the sexton arrived to get his grave digging instructions. Louis 'Kermy' was illiterate. Intelligent and proud first, however, and unable to read or write, secondly. Thus, the priest had made it quite clear before Louis arrived where the plot was on the cemetery plan he showed us and we had sketched it out with exact distances marked from plot and grave site to plot and grave site. When Louis arrived he had to repeat it, however, since Louis was, ostensibly, in charge. While the priest repeated himself and instructed Louis on who to get to help clear snow, break through two feet of frost and, if lucky, dig into some softer gravel to bedrock, we all sipped another cup of tea.

At the cemetery we located the general area and found enough headstones blown clear of snow to measure with Louis' tape. Warmed with ample rum, the temperature seemed almost mild though it was still 15 degrees below.

"Fourteen and six is twelve," shouted Louis, and then quickly, "No, God damn, no, it's...."

"Twenty," Art said.

"Twenty," Louis shouted. Then, measuring another way from another grave site, Art holding one end of the tape and Louis the other, Louis shouted, "Ten and ten is (a pause) is...fifteen," he shouted, just as Art said "twenty."

"Twenty!" said Louis emphatically. "Exactly twenty," he shouted. So it went as we measured and found the site where the grave would be and marked it with the sticks and red flag Louis had carried with him.

Louis was part Micmac and part French. He was born near Black Duck and had no schooling whatsoever, but for thirty years, until his recent retirement, he had worked on the railroad and he'd travelled on the "Bullet" to St. John's and Gander and Grand Falls and Botwood and Port aux Basques and all over. He was a worldly, wise and jolly man, brimming with humour. The funniest, most pleasant, most clever *jackatar* on the west coast, and he loved his priest. Louis took his responsibilities seriously and two days later the grave was ready for the burial. I never could figure out how they penetrated frozen earth almost to bedrock, but Louis knew how.

It was a large funeral for Cormack. So many women there felt so much kinship. Scottish and English wives of Newfoundland servicemen, they had married to come to a cold, comfortless settlement of strangers carved out of the Upper Humber wilderness. Forty acres, a few cleared with the thin soil dozed away; a cold frame of a house, a shallow, dug well that sometimes smelled in summer; a wood stove, oil lamps, sparse furniture and, for many, a child born every year.

The soils were acidic and limestone was seldom, if ever, delivered. Most of the former servicemen had been fishermen, but few knew the soil or how to grow turnip. Life was hard for all, but especially for the wives, and hardship made sisters of these strangers from a home they'd left across the sea and to which they'd never return. One or two made their lives happier, or at least more exciting, they believed, with many men. Most, however, toiled and mothered and wept often when they were alone.

Before and during the funeral, Pearl mothered the children, keeping them at games when the procession rolled by headed for the grave site. She was used to mothering the children since Margaret was quite often ill, and probably had wept much too. Now it was really no different except that Steve was there until the funeral service and there were five cars from Hall's house and Margaret was dead at thirty-seven.

The service at the house was brief, but it was just as well. There were so many there and there was so little room. The casket itself, supported by two linen draped stands, took up a large part of the small parlour and many had to stand, respectfully, in the bedrooms and kitchen.

When the priest's last words were spoken, as he turned to allow Heber and Harold to place the top on the coffin, Steve stepped over to it, bent and kissed Margaret's forehead at the hairline, brushing his lips over the dark black hair, now more perfectly coiffed even than in life.

Later we all stood around the grave site with its frozen soil piled in clumps by the shallow hole. Bedrock was about three feet down from the surface here. This was good for a cemetery in Newfoundland. The casket, with its top firmly held down by two and a half inch wood screws, had been lowered to the rock and Steve, his aging mother and his twin sisters listened to the words of committal and wept. So did I and so did many others from our community.

Friend Art and his lovely wife Edith, kind Heber and his wife Dorothy, Harold and Mrs. White and most all the inside community were there and now as I saw them, I saw them more clearly than I had ever before. Here, on a raw, sub-zero winter day, with my eyes full of tears from sorrow and wind, I saw them. Then I watched as Steve stepped to the grave's edge, knelt on one knee and held a red rose in his hand over the coffin. Tears rolled slowly down his shallow cheeks as he dropped the rose. Bang!

❧

I jumped up in my bed with my heart pounding. Had I been asleep and was this all a dream? Could a rose make such a crash, landing so gently on a pine box?

Bang! Bang! The loose board beneath the overhead clattered now. The wind was gradually picking up. It must surely be a rough night on the water off the Codroy coast, I thought, as I laid back down, snuggling into my feather nest, pulling the comforter about my head.

Steve and I had experienced a lot together in the few years since I'd met him. Once we came close to going for it in a wicked wind trying to make it from Little Grand Lake Brook across the end of Glover Island into the shelter of Dead Head Bay and old Camp 33. We'd just passed two wonderful days around Little Grand assessing marten sign in the big pine and spruce stream valleys and gorges and checking out the high country above the lake. Leaving the old Peterborough at the brook outlet, we built a raft of fir sticks, rope and rabbit wire, to pole across the brook several miles upstream and below the outlet of the lake. We tented just above the outlet falls. It had been a good trip. There had been a good sign of marten and the trout were plentiful.

We knew the wind was strong, but from the shelter of the inlet where the canoe was stashed we couldn't tell just how bad it was. We also knew that Grand Lake was tricky with a strong wind from any direction. The deep cut valleys leading down to lake level from high country and the towering Glover Island funnelled the wind and sometimes the wind would sweep the lake from different directions, coming down these natural tunnels. That's what was happening on the day we chugged out of the inlet with the 4 hp. Johnson, easing our heavy old craft slowly into a raging torrent of water spouts that shook us and beat us as water flooded over the gunnels. It would have been suicide to try and turn back once we were out in it. We had to go ahead, but the old Johnson barely moved us against the wind, so besides bailing with a quart fruit juice tin we had fixed with rabbit wire for boiling up, I also had to paddle! Bail and paddle, paddle and bail, as fast as I could and still we settled low as the bow crashed into the windswept water higher than our heads and flowed over the gunnels into the old square stern.

How we made it God knows, but we did! We had maybe an inch or so of free board showing when we finally made the calmer water of Dead Head Bay, giving me a chance to bail more and paddle less until finally we gained an upper hand. I understood then how others may have erred in judging this water in years past. Several had drowned and others had come close to it around Glover Island.

After that trip, Steve and I always treated Grand Lake with a little more respect, even more than we did other lakes, but all of them deserved our respect and had it. We often headed for shore to wait out a blow and some of our friends should have. It was just a couple of years after our close call near the tip of Glover Island that friends Eric Johnston and Max Rabbits drowned on Serpentine Lake.

The rivers claimed lives, too, of course. Most of the time drownings or near drownings were caused by a split second of carelessness; a paddle or a pole caught for an instant between rocks or an unexpected off-balance from a submerged rock in a run you'd always slipped with ease. Sometimes like with Bill Cormier, who died on the Codroy, no one ever really knew how it happened.

Thinking back to the Codroy again, I remembered my first visit to the weathered grey house Steve had been born and raised in. Mrs. Hall, Steve's mother, was a pleasant lady with her share of wrinkles and greying hair. Short and plump, she was the opposite of the six-foot slender Steve who neighbours said took after his father, dead now for several years.

On that first visit Steve took me down the lane between the riddle fences built to keep the sheep out to Skipper Jim Collier's neat green house nearby. In the skipper's kitchen the old captain offered us rum. Steve's assent was the usual, "Don't mind if I do, skipper." With that he took the rum bottle and poured a dab into a glass, filling the glass up with water from the dipper in a pail by the sink. I saw the dark rum swirl in his glass as he stirred the mixture with a spoon and I thought to myself, "Old Steve must be sick, takin' so little."

I was used to rum, both dark and light, but I had never seen such a heavy rum syrup as this and, sure, I should have known better. Thinking so surely that Steve would have helped himself to more if he'd been feeling well, I poured a half a glass full and topped it off with water. My drink, after stirring, was much darker and thicker than Steve's and I lifted my glass, smiling, took a *big* swallow—and nearly died! I couldn't breathe. My eyes watered. I couldn't speak. I sat and turned my head, looking out the kitchen window as if nothing at all was wrong, hoping they wouldn't speak to me for awhile and hoping they wouldn't see the tears welling up in my eyes.

After the crisis had passed, I sniffed and got out my red handkerchief and blew my nose, brushing the tears away as I did so.

"Bit of a cold comin' on, I guess," said I.

We sat and talked and I took wee small sips of my several hundred (or thousand or more) proof rum. By the time Steve had finished his drink and *turned down* a second, I was about a third through my poison. Fortunately they kept yarning for a while and I had maybe two big swallows left when Steve announced we were going so we wouldn't keep supper waiting. Well, I finished it, again unable to talk and barely able to breathe. After stepping out the door I did, in a sort of hoarse whisper, thank Captain Jim for the drink. He kept a straight face, all right, but Steve had trouble holding back a grin. It was a hazy walk back and a hazy supper I had that night.

❧

As sleep overtook me again I saw a young girl dressed in bridal white, suspended, it seemed, in the air. But soon the vision changed and I saw that the bride sat alone in the centre of a room with empty school desks lining the walls. In a big classroom next door, one with the round parlour stove in the centre, sixty people danced to an accordion playing jigs and reels and "The Star of Logy Bay," while a little classroom on the north side of the schoolhouse served as a kitchen. There, several of the Home and School ladies scraped leftover food into buckets and packed dishes and pans away, bundling them in papers in separate piles and labelling them for their owner. The meal and the toasts were over and the time was under way.

Pearl and I were talking to the bride when her new husband walked in from the kitchen and stood stiffly, putting his small calloused hands on the back of the chair that held his bulging little wife. He was a short, skinny eighteen-year-old, dressed in a tight fitting suit, his first and only suit his father had bought him a size too large, when he turned sixteen. It was now a size too small. The legs and arms were too short and the jacket wrinkled and gathered at the buttoned waist. The crotch was tight, too, and besides the stress and genuine anxiety he suffered emotionally at becoming a husband and a father, all in a matter of days, he was also in considerable discomfort from the trousers that chafed the skin of his perineum.

His bride was not so stressed, but she was sad and also in some discomfort. She was due to have a child and the race to the altar had caused two of her sisters much concern. Etta and Rose had looked forward to the reception with great anticipation and there would have been no 'time' if Dib had the baby too soon.

Fortunately for them and for many others, she didn't, but she was uncomfortably close and now disconsolate at not being able to take part in the grand festivities so joyously celebrated by others in her honour. She wore a lovely old-fashioned white wedding dress, complete with a veil and she clutched a tiny bouquet of wilted wild flowers in her little hand. The dress had been Harry Tole's mother's and that good woman had loaned it before to her own daughters. She could do no less for Harry, and for Dib, whom she and her husband, Uncle George as he was known, would now take in. Uncle George had made Harry do the right thing. Still, there were doubts in the mother's mind that Harry was really the father. To be sure, George had walked in the woodshed one day a few months ago and surprised Harry 'doin' it' to Dib right there on the floor, but she'd heard rumours that there were others too, even though Dib had only just turned fifteen. She knew too about the talk agoing on about Etta and Rose. If her older sisters were 'like that,' God knows Dib probably was too. It had all been a shock to Uncle George and Mary Toles. Their older daughters were chaste and innocent when they were wed, as they expected all their children to be. Uncle George's family was one of a few strong fundamentalist families belonging to a strong Christian group in the area, all known for their hard work and their personal and family discipline. Who would have thought that young Harry would have been the one?

As we stood making slight and simple conversation with Dib and Harry, I thought back to a particular rainy fall day some nine months before and Sheldon, one of the bunkhouse crew whose work I was responsible for.

It had been raining for two days and the Cormack road was a long and treacherous muddy trail. Some of the by-roads were completely mudded in and no rigs at all could move over them. Only people and one dog, Whisky, walked from houses three miles or more from their dead-end turnabouts to the Co-op store and the school. On that particular Sunday afternoon I had gone to see Jimmy Black, our crew foreman, to instruct him to use his park crew inside making tables and benches until the rains left up. To help me in the event I got stuck, I stopped at the bunkhouse for one of the boys to accompany me and Sheldon had volunteered.

I couldn't drive in the yard because of the mud and it was with some difficulty that I even managed to turn the old Fargo around. We had precious little traction in the slithering mud since the truck was empty. It was still too early to add any birch sticks for the winter weight.

Jimmy's truck was in the yard, so we thought he must surely be home. We walked across the road and up to the door and pounded. In a moment a giggling seven-year-old opened the door, giving us shelter from the pelting rain. The room we entered had a space heater, a settle and a couple of wooden boxes that served as chairs and, on that day, also held the five Black children, ranging in age from one to seven. Dib was there too, apparently 'sitting' the babies. She was lying with her head on the arm of the settle, smiling at us, barefoot and with her dress gathered up around her waist. She was, in fact, almost all bare.

"Lordy, Lordy," whispered Sheldon behind me.

"Where's Jimmy?" I asked.

"He's gone."

"Is Meg here?"

"She's gone too. Come on in."

The children were laughing and playing on the dirty floor. Some had dresses on and some had only underwear. The tiniest was naked. They rolled a ball and pulled at the arms of a rubber doll and tussled about with one another.

"Where's he gone and when is he getting back?" I asked.

"They's gone to Deer Lake with Mr. Collier. I don't know when they'll git here, b'y." She urged us again to "come on in and take a spell."

Dib's knees moved apart and back together as she talked, inviting us to stay with her eyes, with her smiles and with her nudity. Poor Sheldon kept repeating "Lordy, Lordy" over and over in my ear.

"Tell Jimmy to wait here in the morning until I come by," I said. "I'll be here before eight." Dib just kept smiling and moving her knees and watching Sheldon. As I turned and opened the door Sheldon was in my way. He was whispering in my ear, imploring me to stay.

"Lordy, man, ain't you goin' to stay?" he whispered.

We walked out through the rain and got in the truck. Poor old Sheldon was beside himself. "I kin take the truck back down after you gets home, can't I, skipper?"

"No you can't! This truck is not going to be at Jimmy's house again today or tonight!"

Of course I knew Sheldon would probably put on his oil skins and *walk* the three miles out and three miles back, but that was Sheldon. Nothing I cautioned would change what he had in mind.

At seven-fifteen the next morning I drove up to the bunkhouse. The rain had mercifully stopped, the wind was cool and from the west, and the clouds were moving rapidly across the face of the sun that occasionally brightened a dreary landscape. Sheldon was frying bologna on the bunkhouse stove and the tea water bubbled on the back. The two other bunkhouse lads had already eaten and were out cleavin' wood, adding to next winter's pile.

"You went back out to Jimmy's," I said.

"Lordy, Lordy," he said, shaking his head. "Why, she hardly had enough heat to draw me off, skipper."

I thought of all this now. Certainly one candidate for 'real father' was Sheldon, who had walked six miles in torrential rain to appease his unconscionable tumescence. But, I knew, and Pearl knew, and all of Cormack knew there were others, just as Mary Toles *thought*. There were a half-dozen husbands and fathers in Cormack and twice as many pulp truck drivers and woods contractors who daily picked up girls along the roads, not just in Cormack, mind you, but all over the west coast. Cormack was not much different nor were the children here any different. There were always some girls, everywhere along the roads. It was, after all, a new and exciting age for the roads had only been in existence in many places for a few years and Cormack, especially, was new—only ten years old, in fact. Some houses had just been built and some by-roads had only been bulldozed clear for a year. In Cormack, walkin' the roads was a girls favourite pastime.

Then the vision changed. I was outside now, behind the parked rigs, relieving myself. It was the same wedding night and Pearl was in talking with Dib and Harry. We'd pulled up a couple of chairs by the hapless couple when the punch I had been drinking pressured me to go outside.

"Come on, Harry, give it to me."

I knew before I walked around the rig I was behind who they were. I was surprised, however, to see two other pillars of the community drinking from quarts of Jockey as they leaned across the back of a half-ton, watching. The time, it seems, was reverting to form. The Tole's elders and their relatives, except for Harry and Dib, had left. The hour at ten o'clock was late for the Toles, and so the beer and, indeed, the rum was beginning to appear. In fact, I'd noticed a change in the sharpness of the fruit punch with my last glass, too. No doubt this was the cause of the increase in noise from the dance hall. Others had discovered the change in the atmosphere this evening long before I had, perhaps.

It was as I had thought, six foot five inch Harry Emmet with his trousers gathered around his ankles and his shirt tail only partly covering his buttocks, moving swiftly back and forth between blond Etta's legs. Her rump was at the edge of the dropped tailgate of a Ford half-ton and she was holding her head and waist angled upward with the help of her elbows. In her right hand she clutched a quart of Jockey and she leaned a little to the left to balance herself as she brought it to her lips.

I stepped behind the rigs and carefully circumvented the group as I made my way back to Pearl, the bride and the groom. I wondered if the two neighbours I'd seen enjoying their beer as they watched would, in turn, allow themselves to become more actively involved, but no matter to me. This was the way things were.

❧

That cursed banging! I was awake again. How many times would I be disturbed with the wind and the flapping boards, I wondered. It reminded me of spring in Cormack when, with two feet of snow still on the ground, a hairy woodpecker began to waken us at daybreak each morning, hammering on the downspout outside the corner of our bedroom. He was, of course, announcing his territory—and disturbing me in mine!

Spring in Cormack meant that the bedclothes no longer froze tightly to the plywood where they sometimes made contact with the outside walls. It meant mudded, impassable by-roads and, if you didn't have fences, either riddle or modern page wire, it meant cows in your garden and horses on your lawn. It also meant you had to exercise extreme caution in driving, for herds of twenty or more horses could cross in front of you in an instant. Suddenly finding your truck in the midst of such a stampede was cause for quick and skilful action, or lacking this, a rapid approach to the Almighty. Spring might also mean dodging sheep on the road on the 'outside' and it did mean it was time to cut birch for the next winter, only a few months away. It was also a time for planning on the part of the growers of root crops and cabbage and much discussion took place seated on sacks of flour and sugar in the Co-op store.

I remember well the morning I entered the store a few minutes past eight and, finding no on behind the counter, had started walking toward the rear of the store when I heard Art sing out, "I'm in here!"

This wasn't like Art, to be in the office at eight-ten, when the half-tons were stopping regularly for gas, or for a drum of oil to be wrestled from the shed, or for a bit of salt meat for the missus. I walked into the little eight by eight room, half-filled by his desk and a wall of shelves. Art was seated behind the desk, leaning back looking straight up at the ceiling.

"Good morning," I said cheerfully. "What's going on?"

Art's voice was fairly high when normal, but when excited it was even higher and now he fairly shouted in his highest voice. "The safe, the safe, look, look. It's gone!" So it was.

Well, it turned out we (the Co-op) lost about two thousand dollars in cash and cheques. Art had called Gerry Mercer on the CNT phone and Cpl. Hogan was soon at the store with Cst. Porter and Cst. Haddad. Wayne Porter and Roger Haddad were mainlanders, but John Hogan wasn't, and from the beginning Hogan had a pretty good idea who the culprits might be. There was talk of making casts of the tire prints, of dusting and printing, and all such good things from the younger men, but Hogan brusquely brushed them aside for more practical things.

"They've got to have dynamite. Go check out Bowater's shed," he said.

For my part, I had a hunch. They'd have to stash the safe before blowing it, some place where they wouldn't be heard. I drove out the road and explored every side road into choppings or into the Cormack burn all the way to Little Falls Brook. Some roads were still impassable so I walked in, checking for tire tracks and footprints. The safe weighed four hundred pounds or more so it would not be carried far. I checked every road until I got right to Little Falls Brook, but that one I didn't check, for the first salmon had hit and there were tents set up just across the brook, and no one in their right mind would blast a safe right across from those tents. But they did!

One other time I chanced to be in the Co-op at a more opportune time. One night we were having a director's meeting, seated on the sacks and barrels in the darkened rear of the store. Only a single 60 watt bare bulb glowing dully hung over the front counter, powered by our pulsing generator, but the light was observed by the driver of a passing car and he had stopped. The man came to the door and knocked loudly, trying the latch on the bolted door at the same time.

"It's Eric Johnston," Art said. "I'll let him in and see what he wants."

While Art went and opened the latch to a grateful Eric the rest of us carried on in the rear, quite out of sight in the shadows at the back.

"Where ya been, Eric?" Art asked.

"Up to Birchy," Eric said.

"Get any trout?"

"Did we? We got over two hundred! I've never had such good fishing at the Duck Hole since I've been in Corner Brook."

"Two hundred!" Art exclaimed. "I wish I could have luck like that. I've never had much more than sticklers on me hook anytime I've gone troutin'."

With the conversation being so interesting, I stood up. By the time Eric got to the door, smiling and happily describing their catch (his partner was passed out on the back seat of his car full of trout and rum), I was standing beside him.

Now one of my responsibilities was to enforce the various fish and wildlife regulations, so when I told Eric I wanted to see his catch, the man was immediately crestfallen, deflated and maybe even heartbroken, for he knew what I was about to do.

Well, you never saw such a mess of mud trout in all your life! With the help of flashlights and new batteries Art provided from his shelf, we counted out one hundred and ninety-five ten to fifteen inch beauties. They'd eaten a few when they boiled up before leaving Birchy. The possession limit was thirty-six each, so they would legally have been entitled to seventy-two, so I counted out one hundred and twenty-three and, with Art's cooperation and help, packaged them and put them in our Co-op freezer for evidence. Poor Eric. He managed the Glynmill Inn for Bowater and he certainly didn't want negative publicity nor did I wish to cause him any, so I agreed that I would ask Cpl. Hogan to call the magistrate in Corner Brook to arrange for Eric to plead guilty and pay his fine out of court. Which he did.

We distributed the trout about Cormack in a few days. Of course, we should have distributed one hundred and ninety-five rather than one hundred and twenty-three, but after that evening Eric was not only a friend but a source of information for those of us serving as Peace Officers.

Yes, I thought, Cormack has many good memories. Still, some are not so great. There was the December Pearl and I decided to return to our families for Christmas, for instance. We not only met with a fierce winter storm trying to get to Stephenville and out by TCA (Trans Canada Airlines), but we met the end of the same storm returning and we met far more. We'd left Steve in charge of the house and our space heater during our absence, but as it turned out, two very different activities enjoined to make out return just a little bit depressing. One of these activities was my own. I had bottled twelve quarts of home brew and left it behind the space heater in our living room. The other had nothing to do with me whatsoever, or so I thought. It was the occasion of one of our neighbours having to slaughter a bull.

As Steve told it afterwards, and as it just *might* have happened (but probably didn't), Gus had asked him to help with the bull and before going to help, the two had gone to our place to check the fire and make certain all was well in the house. As it turned out, Gus' brother, Heber, was on his way home from the local store with a brin bag full of groceries and Gus and Steve met him on the road walking along with Harold Guzzwell, our VLA (Veterans Land Act) representative. After a short discussion concerning the work at hand, all four men entered 'good old Don's' house.

Now most people on entering our living room would certainly have noticed the darkened walls, furniture and drapes. A blow back in the oil circulator had drifted black oil dust into every crack and onto every surface. The place was filthy.

"Look here, Steve, old man, it looks like the stove went up," Harold noted.

All four men examined the room. They observed some soot and they noted that the fire was no longer burning. After close scrutiny and some thought, Steve agreed that the stove had probably caused the appearance of the soot. They also agreed that seeing as how the stove was out and that the wind was still blowing it would be better to wait until the wind died down before relighting it.

This discussion lasted for a few minutes, after which Gus changed the subject by asking, "Where's the brew you mentioned, Steve, old man?" Steve strode swiftly to the corner of the living room behind the heater and opened a cardboard carton. Inside were ten full quarts of sealed brew and two empty bottles. Lifting a full one out, he held it up to the window. Except for the lower inch or so, it was a clear, almost colourless liquid.

"That looks good enough to drink," Heber noted.

Steve nodded and, pointing to the two empties, passed on his expert judgement obtained from experience. "A bit sweet but not a bad drop of brew," he acknowledged.

Harold was a man of action and dwelling on the possible merits or faults of a brew was not a part of his calling. "Gents, let's all have a drink to good old Don!"

Assent was loud and nearly unanimous. Heber was brimful of conscience, however, and through the tinkling of glasses at the end of stretched arms, he made himself heard, if only faintly. "This isn't quite right, is it? I mean, guzzling Don's brew like we kind of plan to do?"

Now the clamour rose to a pitch of ecstasy, all claiming what a swell fellow was Don, how he would want them to have a drop, and besides, "look what we're doing for him, taking care of the fires and all."

Heber was reasonably impressed and adequately convinced. The agreement was now unanimous. A fourth glass, a fourth smile, and the bout was on.

It was half-past one in the afternoon when the jolly boys left our house. The fire was still out and any thought of re-lighting it had faded with the rising physical glow germinating now deep within the bowels of each of our four friends.

The job at hand had not been forgotten, however, and Gus was now solidly behind the idea of all four musketeers taking part in the killing of the bull. "I'll bring the gun out and each of you fellows can have a shot," he suggested.

"Steve can do the honours," Harold said, "but I will gladly stand by to mention a few parting words of grace for the decreased."

Heber was in full agreement with what anyone said now, for he was not used to imbibing as heavily as were his partners in crime. Of course, Gus was in agreement, for most of all he wanted companionship, comradeship and fellowship on this occasion which he so deeply dreaded.

As the four men entered the barn, the bull rose to meet them as if honoured by such a visit. The men gathered round his stall and laid out plans.

"There she is," Gus announced, "we got to kill him, Steve, old man."

"He's going to a better world, a far far better world than ours," droned Harold. "He's to be killed just for a few nasty old juicy steaks. And on your plate, too." He looked at Gus. "What a shame."

The firearm was old. It had no markings on it and Gus claimed it was an old American Army rifle, and maybe so. It was a bolt action design, single shot, and at present was held together by some wire around the barrel and forehand rest.

Gus produced a half-dozen fat, formidable looking cartridges and he handed them to Heber. It was maybe a 44.-40 or 38.-55. "Here, you can be the ammunition carrier," he announced.

Relieving Gus of the rifle, Steve asked, "You want to shoot him here?"

"Hell no," cried Gus, who proceeded to open the stall gate. Whereupon Harold leaped for the ladder leading to the mow, but was coaxed back as the docile creature allowed itself to be lead into the barnyard, seemingly pleased with the attention from its newfound companions.

The stage was now set. Everything and everyone was ready. Placing a cartridge carefully into the breech, Steve closed the bolt, brought the rifle to his shoulder and took careful aim at the bull's head, between the eyes, one foot away. The bull stood quietly, facing them, expressionless, as bulls often are.

"I can't bear to look," Gus said, turning his head and covering his eyes. He meant it.

Heber stood watching. "I believe that bull's been drinking," he said. "Look how blurred he is."

Steve smiled, became more serious, levelled and squeezed. "Click" went the gun and the bull blinked.

It took a moment for the shock of the unexpected stillness to penetrate. After an interval of a minute or so, four suggestions came almost simultaneously!

"Shell's a dud!" "Firing pin worn!" "Hammer only let down to half-cock!" Then "I missed," said Steve. "Here, you try it," and he handed the relic to Harold.

Harold now loaded the rifle and took careful aim. The bull remained stationary, peering sleepily at his executioners. Gus turned away again and Heber had nothing to say. Steve stared wonderingly. "Click" went the rifle.

Heber said he saw the bull smile this time, but a discussion was called for and the troop departed for Don's house, where they talked it over until sometime after 3:00 p.m., by which time the brew was nearly finished. They returned to find the bull peacefully munching a mouthful of hay and as the men approached he didn't even bother to glance around at them. He was used to his friends now.

A conference was held at the fence. The bolt was removed from the rifle and replaced, the shells were examined and everything was pronounced to be in working order. This was to be a final attempt with the rifle which, if it did not succeed, would be replaced by some other method, preferably an axe between the eyes, wielded by Heber. Steve was elected to do the honours once again. Lifting the firearm up carefully, he aimed again at about twelve inches and squeezed.

"Blam!" The blast shattered the air to bits and the bull crumpled.

The boys had left me with two quarts of brew and left Pearl with a dirty house. I don't recall getting a steak from the bull, if there ever was a bull.

Alcohol had good effects, too, however. There was the Friday night, for instance, that a neighbour asked if I would drive our '51 Chev for their family at the funeral on Sunday or Monday, depending upon "when Uncle John died."

"Of course," I said. "I'll be ready and we'll have the car clean and neat." Since there were only two cars on the inside, the Taylor's and ours, we were called on to carry bereaved families fairly often.

Mostly the vehicles in Cormack were half-ton rigs except for three or four farm trucks and a couple of pulp trucks.

Well, the neighbours didn't come and about ten days later I was steering the Fargo among the ruts, headed for Deer Lake, when lo and behold, there was Uncle John beside the road, waving his hand in the direction I was headed! It was cool and damp with easterly winds and fog so thick in places you almost had to poke a hole to spit. Uncle John was wearing a wool cap with a visor, a high neck wool "ram fuck" sweater over his shirts, wool pants and oilskin boots as he crawled up into the cab with me.

"Uncle John," I said, "I thought you were supposed to die last week."

"No b'y," he said, "de doctor tol' Gard de ole man wan't goin' ta live so's he might's well have some rum if 'e want it, so's Gard gie me rum, b'y. Dat's what did it, b'y. It was de rum!"

As others have noted before me and will again, life was so much fun living for those fortunate enough to be rural or outport Newfoundlanders then that few paid much heed to dyin'. It was, after all, just a part of livin'.

❧

The crackling of a good fire and the smell of coffee, bacon and beans slowed my thoughts a bit now. It was morning and I hadn't slept a lot, though I had dreamed much. The wind had died too and the clanging and banging had ceased. I knew Steve was preparing a hearty breakfast that I would enjoy with him and his mother.

❧

That long night in Codroy was more than thirty years ago now. Steve only had a few years of livin' after that night. He died, too young, of multiple heart attacks just as he and his newly found life partner, Vange, were 'livin' fine.' Steve had a productive career in the early wildlife days of Newfoundland beginning in 1951 when Doug Pimlott first hired him as an assistant. He was competent in the country and around a camp. He was also the most graceful fly caster I've ever watched and he tied beautiful flies. I still have in my fly box what's left of a number eight double hook 'blue charm' he tied. He tied it for me one evening after we'd landed five big grilse two miles down from old Camp 37 on Adies Stream.

New Car

The day the car came Bouche was working in the woods, but his wife was home and she signed the papers with her 'X'. This seemed to the salesman just as good as having Bouche sign with his 'X' since the car was paid for anyway. Bouche had paid cash for it a month ago and asked that it be delivered as soon as it had been completely overhauled.

It had been completely overhauled. The paint job had been retouched and the car had been cleaned and polished. The 'looking like new' tires were recaps and a tin of 'Motor Rhythm, the complete motor overhaul magic fluid' had been sloshed through it. The crankcase was filled with oil just a bit too heavy for normal use and though the front end wasn't too secure, the head mechanic at the garage felt that with Bouche's lack of experience behind the wheel, he would never notice a little wandering.

There she sat! Five hundred dollars worth of Chev that looked like new, right there in Bouche's front yard!

Bouche got off the portage truck at the corner late that Saturday afternoon and walked down the road towards home. Slouching along, toeing in, long arms hanging to the knees, Bouche jogged on, thinking about his car just as he had ever since he bought it.

"Some car she is," he thought. "Yes, sir, it was some Jesus car I bought. She's all green. Shiny and all green, she is. Jesus, will she go! Hah! They'll look at Bouche and say, 'Hey, look at Bouche, look, look. He got a Chevy now!' By God, won't dey look now! Some car! Some Jesus car she is."

It hardly entered his head that he didn't have a license or that he didn't understand the barest fundamentals of operating a car. He'd never driven nor had he paid much attention to anyone else when they were driving. After all, the roads had only been built a few years ago.

Bouche turned to enter his drive and, catching sight of something green, he suddenly felt weak and trembly like all over. There she was! He grabbed the gatepost to steady himself as he collected his thoughts. "What to look for? What to do? My Jesus, dere she is!"

For a minute he stood there shaking. He had never felt so weak before.

Down at the store that night Bouche stood sort of propped up against a pile of brin bags. That was a night! A real night, he thought, and he stood there waiting.

Sammy Allan came in with his cross eyes focusing and flashing at people he wasn't looking at and a half-smile on his face that bespoke of chronic complaints.

Bouche didn't often speak first to anybody, but tonight he smiled broadly, jerked his head upward in recognition and spoke quickly. "Hi, Sam," he said.

Sam strolled over, hands in his pockets, for a short conversation with Bouche. Both men were of French origin from down the coast and had settled here to farm and cut pulp after the War.

"Where you working at now, Bouche?"

"Camp 106," said Bouche with a broad smile, as if it was actually a particularly happy place to work out of.

"Comin' along good wit da cut?"

"Yeah," Bouche nodded, still smiling.

"You got a chain saw, have you, Bouche?"

"No," he answered, still with his expectant smile.

"Excuse me, dere's Duffy and I got to see him before he leaves."

"Sure," said Bouche, his smile now gone.

Bouche scratched his head and shoved his cap back. His dark face and deep brown eyes looked thoughtful. "Whyn't Sam mention de car? Sam's a good fella," he muttered softly to himself.

Bouche waited against the pile of brin bags. It was only eight o'clock and there would be plenty of people comin' in yet tonight. Surely someone would mention his Chev. But his face beamed smiles and portrayed wonder alternately all night. With each new customer Bouche felt he had a feeling of kinship when they entered. By the time they had bought groceries and left, however, the feeling had faded and he felt very much alone.

The store closed at 9:30 and Bouche waited by the brin bags until the last customer had gone. The store manager was last to leave and Bouche went outside with him.

"Anything special you wanted?" the store manager asked.

"No."

"Could I give you a lift home?"

"No. I got a car."

"You have?" the store manager was truly surprised at this. "Where is she?"

"Home."

"I'll run you over anyway," said the manager. "What kind of a car have you got?"

"A Chev!" Bouche beamed. Here was a man. Here was a friend. Here was a brother even. "You de only one who ast me 'bout her!"

"When did you get her?"

"Tonight," beamed Bouche.

There were other questions the manager could have asked then, but he felt he already knew the answers.

It was weeks before Bouche drove the car. He worked in the woods the whole time and came home only on the weekends. On these weekends he would take time out from getting his winter's wood supply to slip in behind the wheel of the Chev a few times during the day and pretend he was whipping down the Corner Brook highway. He'd turn the wheel sharply going around curves, leaning with her. Then suddenly he'd slam on the brakes to stop for a car or a moose on the high road.

Sometimes Bouche would get out to argue with another driver and then, after establishing his point, crawl majestically back under the wheel of his Chev and resume his trip, shifting gears recklessly with or without the aid of the clutch.

After arriving at Corner Brook, Bouche would slam on the brakes, get out and meticulously inspect the Chev stem to stern, underneath, under the hood and along the sides. He would crawl under the gas tank to make sure she wasn't leaking, crawl under the front end and note the size of the drop hanging from the oil pan, poke his head under the hood and pull the fan belt around a few times and often end up with a close inspection of the equipment in the trunk. After the inspection, he'd leave the car and cleave some wood. This was the business he must attend to. Then he'd return to the Chev for the drive on to St. Georges or back home.

The day came, however, when Bouche really drove the car. It was a Thursday and Bouche was going to Corner Brook and Bernie and Paddy Stroud were going along with him. They were going because they had things to do in Corner Brook and because Bouche needed a licensed driver along, or so he'd been told.

Bernie convinced Bouche to let him take the car out on the highway so that the gates, fences and driveway culverts along the by-road might be avoided. Bouche agreed to this and sat nervously watching Bernie operate the Chev smoothly and effortlessly out to the main road. Bernie and Bouche changed seats. Bernie went over the operating techniques carefully and Paddy repeated them while Bouche sat behind the wheel fingering the gear shift, the wheel and the handbrake. He knew Bernie and Paddy were talking, all right, but he really didn't hear them.

To say that poor Bouche drove erratically would be kind. Actually, he drove sort of spasmodically. The car started, jerked and stalled; started, jerked and stalled. Sometimes she jerked backward and sometimes she jerked forward and sometimes almost straight up. She snorted, groaned and coughed—and when she occasionally finished trembling and settled nicely on all four wheels, Bouche would begin a series of commands resulting in the same spasms all over again.

Finally, after much effort, the car went through a series of forward movements with the motor running. These progressive movements were each terminated, however, after gains of only a few yards by a sharp stab against the brake peddle and the wheezy stalling of the engine.

Steering also posed a problem and Bouche began to wonder after a while how a car could stay within the confines of parallel ditches only thirty feet apart.

It was almost an hour before the Chev was moving slowly down the dirt highway (in one direction). Bouche was driving carefully and the speedometer registered 15 mph. With both hands on the wheel, he concentrated solely on keeping the Chev between the perilous moats on either side of the road.

By this time Bernie and Paddy were badly shaken and weary. Their necks were stiff and sore from constant losing bouts with the physical laws involved and their stomachs were also somewhat unsettled. Both were now sitting in the back seat, trying to relax, hoping, even praying, for the best.

Somehow they made it through Deer Lake and on to the Corner Brook highway. Bouche had so far navigated the vehicle over the Humber River bridge, around curves, over hills and through the village. All of this, everything, he had done successfully. Maybe, Bouche thought, maybe he was a good driver, maybe even a very good driver. He had so far driven fourteen miles without an accident!

Bouche began to feel a little bit cocky now. He thought of going fast, real fast. As the thought matured, his knees became weak and prickly, his head whirled, his pulse quickened.

Suddenly, Bernie and Paddy were aroused from their lethargy. A quick, forward spurt of the Chev had put a light pressure on their chests and their stiffened necks drew back involuntarily. The car was moving now, all right! It was doing sixty and the speedometer needle was still creeping up.

Bernie looked over the seat at the dial. Seventy now and still going! Bouche was pushing against the wheel, forcing himself back against the front seat. His legs were almost rigid. One foot held the accelerator to the floor and the other held the dimmer switch in. Beads of perspiration showed on his forehead. His mouth was closed tightly and a faint smile appeared on his face. He clenched the wheel emphatically, even triumphantly, with a grip that turned his knuckles white. There was no doubt about it. Bouche was aiming to go just as fast as the Chev would take him.

Bernie cleared his throat and tried to talk, but nothing came out. Now they were doing ninety and suddenly Bouche cried out loudly, "Go like shit!"

Bernie was shocked into action. "For God's sake, Bouche, stop!"

The strange voice penetrated the dream and Bouche relaxed. In fact, he relaxed almost completely. He was sweating profusely and he felt all weak and shaky. He slowed her down to sixty-five, a veritable snail's pace after the 90 mph spurt. The road was crooked here and very rough, but Bouche didn't slow her any more. It hardly seemed to him that he was moving now, although he was certainly busy and even somewhat confused trying to handle the car around the many turns, keeping her between the ditches.

They did, however, arrive safely in Corner Brook. By the time they got there Bouche had relaxed his original grip on the wheel and was practising a 'finger tip control'. Bernie and Paddy, perhaps wisely, decided to remain in Corner Brook overnight. Late in the afternoon, Bouche whipped his Chev back toward home, all alone.

❧

Neighbours and friends listened with interest to the Gerald S. Doyle News Bulletin that night on hearing that Bouche had completely demolished his vehicle just outside Corner Brook. Bouche wasn't hurt and the RCMP said that a tie rod had broken or something to that effect. At any rate, a couple of wheels had rolled off while the car was moving at a fairly hight rate of speed.

Bernie asked Bouche about the accident a couple of days later, but Bouche was far from dejected and seemed to be looking ahead with optimism. "Smashed to God-damn pieces, she is. Gonna git a Stoode-baker next," he announced emphatically.

And so he did.

Part II

Yarns from the Outports

The Sea

To most people who only vaguely know about Newfoundland, perhaps Canadians from the country's great cities or almost anyone from the States, the sea is at the heart of Newfoundland and her people. So it was and often still is. Here are three glimpses of the joining of the sea and the people. Friends who appear are Doug Pimlott and Captain Harry Walters. All other names are fictitious.

The Maude Best

Every outport has its crib champion and one summer day in 1955 Doug Pimlott and I took our woods packs from the half-ton and deposited them on the steps of one of the champions who lived on the western Avalon. Cribbage was both a pastime and an obsession for many who filled their evenings honing skills, anxious for the next challenge from a visitor or a friend from a nearby village. There were always some who discounted the skills of the self-appointed champion no matter who claimed the title, of course, and so some communities had more than one champion.

On our third night, after Doug had dropped a crib game to our host and after four of us had finished several spirited games of 120, I first heard the stories of Downey and the *Maude Best* from the skipper. That day I had walked along the bluffs and through the bogs to Lears Cove and back. Somewhere on the marshes along the way I had examined a cairn which I was curious about and so, after we'd finished cards I asked about it.

Now every outport also has a ghost or at least a ghost story, just as it has a champion cribbage player. Just as some have more than one who lay claim to champion so do some have more than one ghost story. Many such yarns have to do with phantom ships or burning ships or wrecks that disappear from a solid storm-washed berth on the beach. They have been told and passed down for generations in isolated coastal communities and in many cultures around the world, but perhaps there have been more such stories put to paper from Atlantic Canada than from any other region. As the Missus brought us tea and biscuits, the skipper told me about the cairn.

He had, he said, along with Father Dolan and others, found Downey himself, and Mrs. Downey too, "out over the mesh [marsh], 'bout 'alf way to Lears Cove." The very next day, he said, they had all returned and built the cairn from rock they hauled up from the shore, for right there where Downey had lain there was no rock to build with. But the story he told was not just about Downey, it was about a meeting near Downey's cairn, a meeting between a strong and simple lad from Lears Cove and three strange men on a stormy Tib's eve.

❧

A westerly gale whipped across the bay this night. Winds to sixty lashed the rocky coast of Cape St. Marys piling sea waters high on the bare-faced cliffs. There are no cliffs to stop the winds here. At the level of the shallow soil where the sheep trod the sedges in summer, there is but tuckamore and scrub to brave the weather; nothing else grows. In the village a few houses shed the wind as it strikes, but the wind welds together again on passing. Snow was falling this night too. Great white tufts almost touched in the air, blurring the blackness with white.

At St. Brides it was the night of the annual parish Christmas party. Outside the hall the roar of the sea pounding against the rocky shore dominated the night sounds and deadened the howl of the wind. Those braving the storm walked in groups, huddled to protect the young and shouted to one another as they picked their way toward the gleaming window of the parish hall. Inside, the hall was gaily bedecked with tinsel, ribbon, balloons and a Christmas tree and all the merry trinkets which go to decorate a hall at a time such as this. A warm fire spread its heat from a long, low stove in the centre of the hall. Children filled the building with tinkling cries, laughter and boisterous shouts. Grown-ups called to one another, shouted directions and asked for help to do this or that to begin the evening's festivities. It takes more than a storm to keep people home from such a party. Tonight meant a hot soup supper, children's verses and carols, games and Santa Claus and, finally, the Christmas dance to the music of accordion and fiddle. No doubt there would be a drop to drink tonight, too, for no party went by without one and tonight most especially called for a nip to warm the heart, mellow the spirit and thicken the blood for the jog back home through the storm.

One man came all the way from Lears Cove to celebrate tonight. Five miles across the marshes he walked, the wind on his left all the way. He knew the path, this man, and he knew the cliffs that dropped 150 feet to the sea. In all the land there was no one stronger or more powerfully built. One of the brothers from Lears Cove, Christopher, was six foot two in height. Broad and of great strength, slow to anger, kindly and dull he was. Only his older brother, Thomas, was stronger than he and some thought the difference in strength none to great.

Tonight it was Christopher's mind to keep a sharp eye out for a lass; one who might be a prospective bride to live with him at the cove. Only a month ago Thomas was married and now he had asked Christopher to get a wife too. This was the right thing to do. One woman living with two men sometimes got lonesome. Christopher was lonesome, too. He had never experienced a lonesome feeling before, but he did now. As the weeks went by the lonesome feeling seemed to grow worse so after explaining to Thomas he went in search of a wife. Ordinarily, both Thomas and Christopher came to the times at St. Brides but now being married, there was no need for Thomas to leave the cove, so Christopher came alone.

The evening began with a children's concert, monologues, dialogues, solos and duets, group singing, plays and the awarding of church prizes. After the concert came the soup supper and then Santa Claus, the evening's climax. At eleven o'clock the dancing began. Some of the little children were bundled up and guided home, but most of them stayed this one night of all the year to watch the grown-ups perform and act just a little like children themselves.

That afternoon, before the rising wind, a Placentia Bay schooner had left the harbour at Placentia en route to St. John's, loaded with fish. They would sell her cargo in town and return with bundles of Christmas gifts for the good people of the settlement. On board the *Maude Best* was a crew of three; the brothers Gilbert and one William Rolls. Between them they had over $2000 belonging to the folks of Placentia; this, plus the fish. Shortly before midnight a young fellow looking out of one of the hall windows at St Brides, to appease a disheartened attitude brought on by the fickle behaviour of his lady friend, spied the faint glimmer of a schooner's running lights. Calling the discovery to the attention of one of his friends, the second lad said,

"She's the *Maude Best*. The radio mentioned her leaving Placentia this evening. Call Uncle Tom." Turning, he searched the swirling crowd. Soon, a sprightly, bald-headed skipper came bouncing along, pipe in his mouth and a lass in his arms.

"Uncle Tom! Look here! Look out on the water."

Uncle Tom didn't like to be interrupted from his dancing, but with a gentle tug or two from the lads he made his way to the window, still holding the lass around the waist with one arm.

"Look! Look at the schooner," the first lad said, pointing to the faint glimmer of her lights.

"She's the *Maude Best* out of Placentia," added the second.

Uncle Tom watched. The lights were sometimes visible and sometimes they were gone. On each crest they shone, but in each trough although they showed they were not seen. "She may make it, but she better put in here," said Uncle Tom emphatically.

In a while, when the music stopped and the dancers rested, several of them gathered about the window to watch.

"She's the *Maude Best*. Uncle Tom says she better put in. What do you say, skipper?"

They talked and as they talked the *Maude Best* cleared the cove mouth, rounded the jutting rocks and disappeared from the watching eyes of St. Brides.

It was one o'clock in the morning when Christopher left the hall. There were many who warned him not to go. The storm had not abated and gusts blew with vigorous fury at irregular intervals. Some asked him to remain and spend the night with them. Storm or not, warnings or not, he went. A strong man, fearless and young, he feared no night and feared no other man. The wind was on his right now all the way except where the trail bent a bit towards the cliffs. At these times the wind drove into him head on. The snow hit him heavily and the flakes became tiny padded blows raining over his body. Christopher walked on, head down, parka tied tightly; over his shoulder his dancing shoes were hung. Sometimes the line slipped down over his arm and he would have to rehang them. A lesser man would have found the walk a struggle, but Christopher's only discomfort came from the occasional gust that blew his breath into the snow-blurred night. At these times he would find it necessary to open his mouth and turn his head just right to catch the wind and then inhale quickly until the gusts subsided.

He knew when he had reached the halfway point. Here, almost three miles from St. Brides, there stood a rock cairn on the open marsh, not far from a small droke of scrub fir and spruce. As Christopher walked by this well-known mark he thought of how it had come to be. It was only six years ago that Downey had left St.

Brides on just such a night as this with two bags of flour. His wife walked with him, carrying only herself as best she could. It was here Downey had rested. He laid down his bags and rested and never rose again. They found his body the day after the storm, the two bags of flour on either side of him. It was not until the following spring that they found Mrs. Downey, however, for she had crawled, half-frozen, into a little droke of wood and partially covered herself with branches she had broken from the trees. They found her in the spring, half-covered, beneath the stunted trees on the edge of the marsh. They placed a cairn here in remembrance of them; where Downey had laid down the bags.

It was while Christopher turned to tack into the wind as the trail bent onto the marsh just below the cairn that, at first, fear gripped him. It subsided quickly though and his body prickled with the sweat that followed, for he could see now that the three figures before him were men. They stood side by side, dressed in oilskins, their hats tied so tightly about their faces and turned away that Christopher could not see them.

"How 'ya gettin' on?" Christopher's voice was swallowed by the wind. As no man answered he felt that they must not have heard him, even though they stood but a few feet away. His second call was arrested by his own choking as the three faces turned toward him. Chalky white, their faces shone, almost glistened! White, surrounded by the black oilskins that blended with the night, they hung alone.

The curse of fear fanned Christopher's frame anew. Unable to move, scarcely able to breathe, his feet were like lead on the snow-covered ground. The prickly sweat was gone now and strength drained from his body, cold as ice. A moment passed. Then the figure in the middle stepped forward and reached his right hand towards Christopher's face. With a quick motion he planted his thumb and first two fingers on Christopher's chin and squeezed firmly. As if from some recess of the great rock shore, a voice sounded.

"You can tell them you saw the crew of the *Maude Best*."

The hand withdrew and the figures moved on together. It seemed as though there was no movement at all as the almost suspended shapes melted effortlessly into the snow and the night. The wind continued to howl as the storm maintained its furry; snow fell as it has been falling. How long Christopher stood, partially dead, he never knew or thought of again. After an unknown time strength began to slowly soak back into his body. Great reserves of energy were released and he ran. His heart beat as the surf pounded and he ran faster now, through snow to his knees, faster than he had ever run before.

It was two miles to the house at Lears Cove. Christopher ran all the way. He crashed through the parlour window and fell sprawling on the floor, trembling, breathless and faint. He drifted into the unconscious amid the shattered glass and splinters from the frame.

On the following day, Thomas emerged from the room where they had laid Christopher. The invalid had regained consciousness during the daylight morning hours and had called for his brother. Now, an hour later, Thomas came out. He sat down heavily by the kitchen table and dropped his shaggy, sweating head into heavy hands. Thomas' wife, a dark-haired, slender lass, more fragile looking than most, sat down across the table from him. Quietly she asked, "How is your brother?"

"He cannot live." Thomas' response was quiet, flat, decisive.

"But why? Why? He was all right just yesterday. Why do you say he cannot live? Tom, my God, what are those marks on his face?"

Thomas looked coldly at his wife. He may not even have noted the hysteria mount and subside as she spoke and his answer was clear; hopeless.

"I know what the marks are, but what he has told me I cannot tell you. Because he has told me, because I know of the marks, I cannot live."

The girl jumped up quickly at his words, startled and frightened.

"But that can't be true. You can tell me. I'm your wife, Tom. For God's sake, tell me!"

He was adamant. "You will nurse us both until death. It will not be long."

She was frantic now. There was no control, no reason left to face the present terror and future uncertainty. Reason was as lost to her as it was to Christopher. She made a final effort, however. She appealed to her husband through a guess.

"It's got to do with the wreck out there in the cove, hasn't it? It's about that schooner that come on the rocks in the night, isn't it? Tell me, Tom!" She screamed her husband's name.

Thomas only looked at her. He didn't speak. He was to speak only once again, to the priest. The distraught woman broke and sobs shook her fragile frame.

The next day Christopher died. Thomas watched him die, but neither man spoke and after death came to the younger brother, the elder leaned back in his chair beside the bed, crossed his legs and waited. Thomas' wife went to St. Brides for the priest. She knew Tom wouldn't go. He was no longer sane, waiting for death there beside his brother.

The priest made the trip to Lears Cove and returned to St. Brides that same day. Upon his return he immediately formed a search and rescue crew to visit the wreck of the *Maude Best*. He sent a telegram to Argentia, informing Dr. O'Brien that one man had died of apparent pneumonia and another was so ill as to be delirious at Lears Cove.

Early next morning a group of men from St. Brides carried Christopher's body across the fateful barrens. Those carrying the home-made coffin expressed the feeling that their burden seemed lighter as they crossed the marsh by Downey's cairn. One made a joke that perhaps the body had got out and run past this spot where the Downeys had lain six years past.

At the church the coffin was opened for the doctor who had now arrived. The bearers wondered what the chalk marks were on Christopher's chin. The doctor stated that he could not state with any degree of certainty what they were, but that they looked something like fingerprint bruises.

Turning to his friend, Father Dolan, he asked, "What do you think, Father?"

Father Dolan, looking steadily into the doctor's eyes, answered, "I believe they are fingerprint bruises, George. The print on the right side is a thumbprint. The two on the left are prints of the first two fingers of a right hand."

Thomas was moved to the Argentia hospital and died a week later of pneumonia. The death certificate of both brothers read alike, although the cause of Christopher's death was somewhat uncertain. For one thing, Dr. O'Brien did not believe Christopher could have died so suddenly from pneumonia. As there were no members of the family living except Thomas at the time of death, however, it was not deemed necessary to hold an autopsy. It was also true that Father Dolan, after viewing the "finger prints" on Christopher's chin, was not sure in his own mind as to the exact cause of death, or even of the delirium in which Thomas appeared to have been in at the time of his visit to Lears Cove. On first observing them he felt that the prints might have been made by the victim himself. Now, however, as he pondered the position of the prints and the story Thomas had told him, he was in doubt. So Father Dolan exposed the strange tale to the doctor and to the police. It was discounted by all as ravings as feverish men.

The *Maude Best* was found to have taken on no water and was in perfect condition except for a split mast. Those who investigated her and searched for the crew and those who salvaged the ship and cargo could give no reason for her mishap on the shoal at Lears Cove. No sign of her crew was ever found.

Oderin

Harry Walters and I had been touring the Avalon and Burin Peninsulas, visiting communities to increase the visibility of the Department of Mines, Agriculture and Resources, a gentle reminder that there was an effort to conserve wildlife as well as eat it. The three-day-tour with Harry ended for him when he left me at Bain Harbour in the care of a Mr. Smith and his son Raymond. I was to travel to Oderin Island and from there to visit other Placentia Bay islands to select one or more for experimental introduction and harvest of snowshoe hares. Harry would return and pick me up a week later if I didn't get storm stayed, in which case he would be waiting in Bain Harbour until the storm was over.

During the past three days I'd had tea and biscuits at Brigus that were better than I'd ever had before or since, and at Cappahayden we sat in the front parlour while two genteel maiden sisters in their seventies made us welcome with their marvellous muffins and home preserves. I felt as though Harry, or Captain Walters as he was best known from his Newfoundland Ranger Force career, must know almost everybody in Newfoundland and that surely everyone *did* know and respect him.

It was during the muffins and preserves in Cappahayden that a three coloured cat with a swollen belly crawled out from under my chair to stretch and wash herself.

"I see," said Harry to the ladies, "that your mother cat is about to have kittens."

Both ladies expressed surprise at this. They looked at each other and back at Harry and after a moment the elder spoke most emphatically and most negatively. "Oh no, Captain Walters, Prissy has never been exposed. She's never been outside this house since we first came by her."

"I thinks," ventured the younger of the two, nodding knowingly, "that she's got a sort of growth of some kind in her."

Harry was always courteous, the model of decorum in the presence of his elders, male *and* female. His handsome mustached face was usually smiling, too, and it was smiling now as he watched a large, broad-faced tom stroll into the parlour from the kitchen. Even with its tail hanging down, the cat's jewels were clearly visible, protruding from its genital region like two gulls' eggs encased in velvet. Harry looked at the tom and pointing at it, said, "But ladies, that's a tom cat!"

Whereupon the elder sister responded with obvious shock, "But, Captain Walters, that's Prissy's brother!"

The mystery might never be solved and compliments on the preserves were in order.

❧

I was now in Bain Harbour and Harry had gone to come back and pick me up on my return from Oderin a week later.

In 1955, Oderin was a community of several dozen families. It was divided into two distinct parts, the Beach and the Harbour. I was privileged to experience both on the several trips I made there over a three-year period. Today, like so many other outport communities, the one on Oderin no longer exists. Its inhabitants were resettled in Burin communities though some have dispersed much further away from their old Placentia Bay home and, of course, others are dead. For me, the island of Oderin held a simple, unique and unparalleled beauty.

I was wondering how in the world the fragile looking little poles held the flakes against the sea. Salt water and wind blew the tiny poles for hours and days and years, but still they stayed. The sea didn't move them, nor did floating slob ice in the spring nor our dory now, as we hit and scraped alongside. My musings were interrupted by a sudden staccato chatter. It came from a clean-shaven, beaming and grinning face looking down upon me. The man had a bald head and a great, toothless mouth that was truly cavernous when opened wide. His tongue seemed to clatter about the opening as he talked and occasionally it flicked out to lick the lips that marked a boundary of the source of chatter and oaths.

"Hello Smith, hello there," he shouted to the skipper who had taken me out from Bain Harbour.

"Hello Harry Converse," my drunken pilot called back. (He was drunk in Bain Harbour when we left and sucked on beer all the way over.)

"Didn't you bring me a bottle of beer, Smith? Hey, Smith," he clattered, "you got any beer?"

Then, as if seeing me for the first time, "Who you got there, John? Who's the stranger? He's not staying with me. We got no room. Smith, you're drunk, you are. Hey look, look, you'll fall out, hang on there, hang on! You drank all the beer, Smith."

Harry Converse's voice was loud. I think people all up and down the Oderin Beach could hear him, even now as we entered his house a hundred yards down the path from the flake and his store. "I brought a strange man, Mary. He's gonna stay here. You got to feed him, Mary. He's come about the rabbits. No need to fuss now. He's gonna sleep in the back room. I got to go now. Caleb Foot, poor Caleb Foot. He died last night. Died with blood running out of his mouth, he did. Now, what do you supposed killed him? Something burst in his stomach, *I* says! He came in yesterday and he had two buoys under his arms and his young fella says to him, 'How are they, old man?'

"'Good for another year, my son,' he says. The young fella turned and he said he thought the old man said something but he was only making noises, the old man was. 'Here,' he says, 'come into the house, old man. It'll pass over.'

"'I'm cruel bad,' the old man says. And he died. Now, what was the matter, I wonder? Something burst in his stomach, I says. I got to go. You get a cup of tea. Mary's coming to see Caleb later. You sit down. Now don't steal our money, now.

"Mary, you give him something to eat now, Mary. He's gonna pay us. Give him something to eat. I'm going to the wake. Poor Caleb Foot died last night."

The woman Mary carried her head tilted a little as if she may have had a slight stroke some time in the past. Her hair was black and her complexion dark. She had, it seemed to me, unusually long arms that hung loosely from her sloping shoulders. Her dress was dark and dirty and her face was drawn and wrinkled. She might have been fifty but she looked seventy. Fore and aft, her body was unusually flat. She scuffed her feet as she walked or sort of shuffled over the floor, waiting on me as I ate.

"A strange man," she said slowly. "Do you like cabbage?"

"Yes."

"He likes cabbage," she said to no one, for there was no one present save we two.

"Do you like pork?"

"No."

"He don't like pork."

"Do you like beef?"

"I like lean beef."

"He don't like fat beef."

When the outside door opened, the conversation, such as it was, stopped. A boy of about seventeen walked in, closed the door carefully behind him and nodded to the woman as he sat down. No one spoke and I continued to eat, although certainly not heartily, for I was beginning to note my surroundings with some apprehension. It wasn't just the woman's dress and her floor that were dirty. It was the tablecloth, the dishes and the silverware as well. I finished trying to eat and sat back from the table. The woman spoke to the young man. "Carl, go tell your mother not to go to the wake without me. I got a strange man here now and I don't want to leave him alone in the house."

With this the boy stood up, opened the door and walked out.

What was this coming in and sittin' and stayin' but never sayin'? I wondered and I recalled the story told me of two young girls who entered the house of neighbour woman one day. After sitting in the kitchen for several minutes and saying nothing, the woman asked, out of curiosity, if they wanted anything. Faced with a direct question, children such as these often move their heads negatively although seldom emphatically. "Are you sure?" In this case, however, the response was more than a head shake. One of the reticent little creatures said quite softly, "Auntie Nita, your house is on fire."

It was and it burned.

As I continued to view my surroundings more critically, I realized that the whole house was really very dirty. The kitchen floor was so coated my shoes stuck as I stood to walk from the table. The walls were grimy with soot and the tablecloth, not just stained but stained repeatedly so that it was a cloth of many colours, was partially coated with grease. The notches in the handles of the woman's tea cups were filled with dirt and tiny particles of food stuck to the plates from one or even several previous meals. She used her skirt to lift the frying pan from the stove and in doing so dipped it into fish grease. Her skirt was also used to wipe her hands, the table and her hands again. Maybe she never removed her dress. I wondered if she even took it off for bed.

When everyone from the Oderin Beach gathered to wake old Caleb I walked over the little island. Leaving the house I passed through the inside and outside gates. From the little fence gates I walked into the road, which was not really a road, of course, since there were no vehicles save bicycles there. It was really only a foot path. To those who walked it daily, however, it was a road and everyone on Oderin walked. The little winding path led along the bottom of a hill, over across a knoll and up the slope above the harbour. Looking down into the water I saw seven schooners at rest along with dories and skiffs. Stages and fish stores surrounded the waterfront and behind these were the houses with a path between. It was the same scene with different coloured houses all around the harbour. Some were yellow, others red or green or blue.

I climbed up higher, leaving the path, and roamed over the little hills of Oderin. The grass was cropped short by sheep and now and then, rounding a boulder or dropping down over a knoll, I would surprise three or four and they would run a short distance away, fearing, perhaps, that they might be caught and shorn again. But I was not a shearer and it was not shearing time. Along the paths made by the sheep I noted many slugs among the droppings left by the animals. No doubt all the sheep here were infested with liver flukes, since both sheep and slugs had existed on Oderin for generations.

I soon found that sheer cliffs dropped 100 feet to the sea around much of the island. All about Oderin other islands of various shapes and sizes were scattered in the sea. They were not now nor were most ever permanently inhabited by humans. Covered with rock, tuckamore and grasses, sea birds nested on them by the thousands and eagles sometimes picked a ledge for their giant stick nests. No doubt there would have been more than a few eagle nests present, but sticks were few and were carried for long distances by the great birds that selected such cliffs as these.

For awhile I lay on the grass, my head against a salt stunted spruce, watching a skiff moving between two islands. The wake for old Caleb Foot was taking up the time and thoughts of all Oderin except the stranger.

❧

Matt Lunn and I lay on the pebbly Jude Island beach, eating sweet biscuits from his lunch.

"There sure is some evil coming in the world."

"It may have always been here," I said. "Maybe we're just beginning to know more about it with our radios and modern communications."

Matt knew of the telephone, magazines, newspapers and even television. He was an intelligent, sensible young man and a hard worker. He listened a great deal to an American Naval Base radio station and particularly liked an American program called *Gunsmoke*. Thin, handsome and quiet, Matt talked seriously most of the time. "It just seems as though one mess gets cleaned up over there and then something else happens. I don't know why people don't get along better. I don't know."

Matt shook his head and stared at a shell on the beach.

"What kind of a shell is that?" I asked.

"We calls it the whore's egg. The priest asked me what one of them was one day and I told him it was the bad woman's egg. I didn't want to say it was a whore's egg and he didn't know the difference."

"I suppose," I said, "that girls leave here almost as soon as the young fellows."

"Sooner," Matt answered. "They leaves as soon as they's old enough to git caught. Some gits caught but more of them nip out in time." He stopped for a minute, perhaps thinking of his own young wife and baby. They had been married in May and now in September had just had their first child, a son, born to them. "I don't blame them, I guess. There's not much here to keep them. If I had a car, I'd leave Oderin."

❧

The breakfast table was covered with litter from Harry Converse's mouth and hands. All about his chair, the floor was covered with bread, pieces of bologna and milk. It wasn't all spilled, for some was deliberately put there. Calling the cats, the skipper tipped up the can of Carnation and poured the thick contents on the floor. Three cats, all dirty grey but presumably all white once, moved to the puddle and lapped it off the floor.

On the evening before we had talked politics, Harry and I. Politics and fish were the subjects most discussed it seemed. Few other topics were considered important enough to spend a great deal of time on, although sometimes when the rum was flowing there was talk of women and sometimes of the war and the submarine that had once surfaced in Oderin's harbour.

"That man Ballam," Harry said, "he must be a good man. They named a bridge after him, didn't they? That's a fine thing!"

They would, of course, never have named a bridge after Ballam if he hadn't done something to warrant it!

"What do we know about politics?" asked Harry, rhetorically, I guessed, since he answered himself. "I suppose," he said, "we knows everything!"

Harry pulled a chunk of bologna skin from his toothless gums with his grimy fingers and said, "I got a letter last year from up where they do the broadcasting. This letter I got, it said, 'What broadcast...' or no it said, 'What news broadcast,' it said, 'is best on the radio for Newfoundland?' That's what it said and I said, *I* said, 'The Doyle, the Gerald S. Doyle news,' I said. 'That's what's best for Newfoundland,' I said. And they sent back and said I was the only one right out of seventeen they asked."

He hauled his hand across his mouth and shook it over the floor, crossed himself and left to do some handlining offshore.

Like other fishermen there, Harry Converse was usually up before dawn. He went out handlining, brought in his catch, split the fish, salted it and went in the house to eat. It was seldom later than one o'clock in the afternoon then. He turned the fish on the flake on some days too, but Mary usually did that job, both of them spitting tobacco juice over the drying cod.

And he also walked over the knoll from the beach to the harbour when the coastal boat came in, to meet it, like the others on the island. Harry's life was orderly.

❧

If you followed the little path over the hill to the harbour, it led you directly to the great white house of the merchant and shipbuilder, fish buyer and fisherman, Lon Dawson. On a later visit to Oderin I had met Mr. Dawson in Bain Harbour and motored with him out between Grassy and Gull Islands across the seven miles of sea to the beautiful entrance of Oderin's harbour. The Dawsons were Protestants. In fact, they were about the only Protestants on Oderin, but there were more than a few Dawsons, for the brothers had families too. I stayed with Lon and his missus. Their lovely daughters were still living at home, but all the rest of their family of six lived and worked somewhere in or around St. John's. The Dawson's home was as spotlessly clean as Harry's house was dirty.

One day as I stood watching the marvel of four men splitting fish over Mr. Dawson's splittin' table, I wondered aloud what the white painted circles were on all the outside doors. They were on the doors of the shop, the store and the two outside doors of the Dawson house. And, though I'd never seen them before, I was to see them often on outport doors later both here and elsewhere.

"Well, I'm not superstitious myself," Lon said, "but others are and my wife is." As he spoke he left the table, threw the split cod from his hand into the handled barrel alongside and moved me over to where the conversation might be more private. If he lowered his voice a little, the others couldn't hear from where we stood, but they did look up, clearly interested in what he might be telling me in answer to my question.

"I've never believed in spirits, but most people believe in them. You've met my brother, George, there," and he nodded toward George, whom I had indeed met a few days before. "George," he said, "is strong on spirits." The two of us were standing right here in this very place splittin' fish years ago when we heard a sound neither of us had ever heard before. We were only boys then. It was a put-put-put sound and it was getting louder, and when I looked out toward where it was comin' from, a boat come around the point toward us. George, he looked up too. There were two men in that boat, just sittin', and we just sort of stared. When one of them stood and waved at us when they got close in, George hollered like he'd seen the Devil and ran as fast as he could away down the lane to his house.

"I never moved, of course. I knew there must be some explanation, but I saw others disappearing from around the harbour, too, and I guess I was the only man that waited to see what would happen."

"What was so strange about it?" I asked.

"Why, it was the first time anyone had seen a dory moving with nobody pullin' the oars! I guess that was the first Acadia engine we'd ever heard or ever even seen. And when they pulled in alongside my wharf there I knew the fellows right off. They'd come over from Boat Harbour just to show us the engine and the boat and how it worked and all. But I was the only man still outside of his house that morning," he said. "Everyone else had run inside and hid."

"Then what are the round, white circles for?" I asked again.

"That's to let spirits go in if they want and get back out if they want. I don't believe in them, but if you don't have a place for them to go in and out when they wants to get in and out, they'll smash a door or a window, maybe, and that," he said, "is a bother to fix."

A Little Blue Mitt

It was a hard life in the outports. Sealing if you got a berth or if you were a landsman and seals were plentiful some springs, some fishing in summer and shooting turrs and ducks in the fall. In the winter, around some of the communities you might catch a few rabbits, and in March month if you lived down north you might kill a caribou. Where there was wood you could cut pulp sometimes too, but mostly your life was on the sea and from the sea.

Today, following the expenditure of millions of dollars, people from another universe, a part of Greenpeace, the International Fund for Animal Welfare and other animal rights and welfare groups, have convinced a part of the developed world that the Newfoundlander's lifestyle was wrong and their culture somewhat less than human. Newfoundlanders have been portrayed as thoughtless slaughterers, wasting a beautiful resource, and sometimes all resources, needlessly. Indeed, the animals have been portrayed as the entity of value, the Newfoundlander's culture valueless and thus a thing to be destroyed.

Powerful lobbies continue to destroy as this is written; they destroy by legal and illegal, often violent, means the lives of people unable to protect themselves; just knowing how to live and how their forefathers lived. Life is so much different for writers in Vancouver or actresses anywhere or for self-proclaimed Messiahs of the wildlife world than it is for the residents of an outport facing the rigours of a Newfoundland winter.

"A Little Blue Mitt" is a simple story of a good people in a Newfoundland outport. It is also a story of a tragedy like real tragedies that happen now and have happened in the past; sometimes, in some years, with uncommon frequency as the weather and the sea determined.

Life has changed a bit today, though people from these villages along the coast of the Northern Peninsula still fish and hunt and snare rabbits, but go back to River of Ponds or Eddies Cove or Castors River for the winter. You go and stay and leave your conveniences, your bank account, the daily paper, your cable TV and all the wonderful appliances and gadgetry and move into a house in 1953, soon after Confederation, and spend the whole winter there!

❧

Corporal Tom stood in the parlour window looking at scads of snow. So far there was no wind. Just big, fluffy flakes—like cotton, falling from a heavy, grey, matted sky. Vic would certainly make the trip to the Bight this evening. There were two sick people to take to the cottage hospital and he wouldn't wait 'til morning. The snow could prevent the trip by then. Besides, tomorrow was the Sunday after Tibs' Eve and though Vic wasn't adverse to returning home on a Sunday, he never felt like venturing away on the sabbath. If he didn't come today he'd bide at home.

At quarter past one Tom checked his watch. Vic should stop around two. The thought that he really should stay until Monday and take the prisoner to the Bight himself was growing stronger. Constable Phillips was bringing him all the way from down northern Labrador and could get home by early morning, Boxing Day, if the corporal was on hand at the Pond to relieve him of the prisoner.

Watching the snow and thinking, Tom's problem thoughts drifted for a moment, replaced by memories. Memories of lines he had once known.

"White as the pure driven snow," he thought, "lily white or pure white, something to do with purity and snow. What was it?"

Trying to recall, to go back so many years, his thoughts stopped at a passing image, something related, a vision of his Alice Marie. He saw her now, all dressed in white.

"Only another year and first communion for her! How much time and how many struggles had been left behind since baby Alice? Now there was baby John. What a hell of a place to 'bring up' a baby, at the Bight! Even little Alice had been better off across the Straits in the Harbour at his old detachment. The bight held nothing for children, babies or for that matter for grown-ups!"

A noise disturbed his thoughts as Mrs. Lonze came into the room. He turned and smiled at her.

"I'm leaving when Vic comes, Mrs. Lonze," he said, "we'll settle up the bill now, can we?"

Mrs. Lonze was Mrs. Lonze (Lozange) Pardy, but everyone called her Mrs. Lonze because Lonze Pardy had several brothers and cousins scattered about the Pond and all up and down the coast, and to keep the womenfolk separate, everyone addressed them by their husband's first names. She was a hefty, large bosomed, red-cheeked, smiling and kindly woman, Mrs. Lonze. Even though she didn't regularly keep boarders, she always saw to it that the RCMP "boys," as she called them, "got taken care of right" when any of them called in at the Pond. She wanted to "keep them first rate," she'd say, if she had anything to do with it.

"Now, Corporal, you come in the kitchen. 'Tis almost Christmas now, and I wants to give you something for your family."

Mrs. Lonze walked into the kitchen with Tom behind her. His thoughts wandered to Phillips for a moment again and it seemed to him now that maybe Phillips would stay here at Mrs. Lonze's over Christmas anyway. He wasn't married and this was as good a place as any for a single man leading a chaste existence to spend the yuletide. Phillips could bring the prisoner right to the Bight Christmas Eve and return to the Pond Christmas morning to spend the day with the Pardy clan, weather permitting. He felt relieved a little now and his mind was made up. "I'm leaving as soon as Vic comes by, Mrs. Lonze. Shall we settle up now?"

The woman eyed him intently. "So you just said, Corporal, so you just said."

The kitchen table was covered with examples of Mrs. Lonze's handiwork. She was a splendid craftswoman with knitting needles or a crochet hook. Little beaded place mats, finely crocheted scarves, knitted wool muffs, socks, mitts, and other items lay on the table.

"I makes a few things through the year for Christmas time," she said, "it sorta saves on the pocket book, not a comin' all to once, like. They're mostly things that our relations can use, ya know."

She looked at Tom and spoke emphatically. "Now, Corporal, I wants you to pick out a gift each for your wife, little Alice and the baby, and you ain't payin' for them either! You just give them to them and say nothin'!"

It took some coaxing on her part, but finally the corporal picked out a set of heavy mats for hot dishes for his wife, a little scarf for Alice and a pair of blue mitts for baby John. He settled up with Mrs. Lonze, tipping her liberally, and packed the newly acquired gifts into his woods pack along with the rest he carried on his winter trips.

Vic stopped the snowmobile in front of the house at two o'clock and Tom rushed out as the horn blew. Couldn't keep hospital patients waiting! Had to be ready always!

Lonze Pardy, running from a nearby house, called to him now, before the door of the big blue Bombardier could be opened.

"Hey Corporal! Here!" Tom waited a moment as Lonze came huffing to a halt. "Here," he said, "take dese rabbits. I didn't expect you'd be leaving' so quick. They'll make a scoff for you and the missus."

Vic was in a hurry and the nurse inside the snowmobile added to his tension by peering out anxiously at Tom and Lonze Pardy. The corporal thanked Lonze, took the brace of rabbits and shoved them inside his pack. He climbed in and slammed the door. They arrived safely at the Bight at six-thirty in the evening. They had travelled the old dog team route behind the bays and bights most of the way after darkness had fallen. But this was nothing to either Tom or Vic. They knew the way.

Tom considered himself rather a disciplinarian with his children. His love and affection was meted out regularly but in small quantities, for time didn't usually permit him to spend whole evenings with his family. Now this Christmas Constable Forward was on holidays and even on the coming Tuesday, the holiest of days, Tom would have to remain on duty. To Alice, his oldest child, this was a little difficult to accept.

"Daddy, will you go across the harbour with us Christmas Eve?"

"No, Alice, Daddy has to stay here."

"But why, Daddy?"

"Because Constable Phillips is bringing in a prisoner on Christmas Day." Tom looked up at Marie for a moment and then turned back to Alice. "He stole somebody's money, so he has to pay for what he did, honey."

"But, why Daddy, why did he steal some money? Didn't he have any of his own?"

"No, dear, I guess he didn't. Sometimes people who have very little of all the good things in life forget that they should be thankful even for that very little bit they do have. It is not as easy for these people to resist temptation as it is for us, honey."

"Oh," said Alice, "why don't they think of the Baby Jesus, then, so they wouldn't steal, Daddy?"

"I don't know, honey but no, I guess they wouldn't steal if they thought of the Baby Jesus."

Alice thought for a moment. Her face brightened and her eyes twinkled. "But, it's easy for us not to steal because we don't need to and we think of Jesus, don't we?"

Baby John interrupted the conversation at this point by falling from a chair he had been climbing up from the back side and upon hitting the floor, crying a little bit louder than the hurt required.

The corporal picked him up and, unable to quiet him, was about to turn him over to his wife when he thought of the rabbits. Holding the howling two-year-old in one arm, he opened the pack and removed them. He quickly covered the pack flaps over the knitted gifts. Spying the bunnies through his tears, the baby's howls soon subsided to whimpers and shortly young John was pulling the fur from the rabbits in his father's hand.

"Oh, for heaven's sake," Marie said disgustedly, "look, look, Tom, he's getting his hand all blood!"

"Where'd the blood come from?"

"From the rabbits, look! The jays must have picked them."

She took the child away from his father and the blood and the rabbits and this being a good excuse to wash, she continued with the two children, preparing them for bed. The hour was late and it was well past their usual bedtime. Both parents heard the children's prayers that night, although this was not a usual practice, for Tom was really not accustomed to such tasks. Tonight, however, he just went ahead and listened and prompted as if it was his practised duty.

With the children safely tucked away, Tom and his wife discussed their Christmas plans. He would have to remain at the Bight certainly. The prisoner would be there until Thursday when Constable Brainard would call, weather permitting, and pick him up. Marie would take Alice and little John and go across the harbour to Tom's sister's. The church Christmas party was being held on the west side this year; it was on the east side last year. The children could attend the party this way and then have a nice Christmas morning at Aunt Joan's with their three little cousins. Then, on Christmas afternoon, the family would return with Father Rooney when he came back. Such an arrangement would give the children a family Christmas and still allow Tom to be on hand any time Phillips arrived.

"With the frost, the slob has cut over solid now, Marie, although it's a bit rough. There's no swatches. Father Rooney has been crossing by komatik since last week, so I'll get Louie to take you over with his team and them come over after you."

Marie nodded assent. It wasn't often these years that the bight itself frosted over solid so early, but this year had been much colder than other winters she'd known here.

With the plans settled and the children safely in their beds, she now began to unburden her mind by questioning her husband for the reassurance she knew he would provide.

"What about the prisoner, Tom? Is there anything to become upset or worried about?"

"Suspected of murdering his uncle for $2000. He'll be held on a possession charge for the present, I guess."

Marie was satisfied. She seldom discussed Tom's work with him and he never mentioned anything to her. It just seemed that at this time of year....

"Did you get a chance to pick up anything for the children? The *Ranger* won't be in now until after Christmas and our big Eatons' order simply won't be here!"

Tom went to his pack. He took out the hot dish mats first and gave them to his wife. "Mrs. Lonze made them," he said plainly. Then, defensively, "I've got an order coming aboard the *Ranger* too, honey."

He smiled at Marie now and she smiled back as she looked at the mats. "What about the children?"

"I picked out this scarf for Alice and these blue mitts for John," he said, handing them to Marie.

"Why, they're lovely! The little reindeer design on the mitts is lovely! But, John, one of the mitts is soaked with blood! Tom, you put those darned rabbits in on top of the mitts and one got soaked with blood!"

The afternoon before Christmas, Marie, Alice and baby John got on the big komatik Louie LeBlanc owned and Louie packed all the Christmas gifts around them. The big point blankets were tucked in and the mixed breed team of sled dogs pulled away. Louie had every breed of dog but a crackie, it seemed, but they were good dogs. Tom waved and called "Merry Christmas" until he knew they could not hear him and only just barely see him. He had made the parting as brief as he could. He disliked partings and emotion only detracted from doing one's duties properly. A kiss and a smile to each child. A long kiss and a whispered "I love you" to Marie. Standing watching, he realized now they could not hear him because of the dogs as well as the distance. In fact, he could barely hear the dogs himself.

There was little time to think of his family, however, for upon returning up the slope to the office he was greeted by Constable Phillips in the sartorial red used on prisoner escort. The prisoner was cuffed to Phillips and was only seconds behind Phillips in wishing Tom a "Merry Christmas."

Phillips left that same night with Vic who had visited the hospital and the mission and decided to return Christmas Eve instead of Christmas morning. As Tom had figured, Phillips would spend what would surely be a festive Christmas with the Pardys at the Pond. Oh, wouldn't he have a scoff, though! Surely Mrs. Lonze would outdo herself on Christmas!

The prisoner was locked in the basement cell. He seemed like a good sort. Tom had questioned him in his brusque manner and the prisoner had answered him slowly, thoughtfully and, apparently, earnestly.

Outside it was getting warmer. The air was no longer frosty and had the feel of rain. A mild was coming after three weeks of cold, a mild for Christmas.

Christmas morning the air was like spring. The thermometer read 56 degrees at seven in the morning outside the detachment door after an all night rain. The corporal went about his duties as he would any other day. The prisoner was fed and remarked that the Mountie was a pretty good cook. They wished each other another "Merry Christmas."

Shortly past noon the barking of dogs brought Tom to the porch. A komatik and team stopped at the steps. It was getting sticky out now and snow was clinging to the runners. The crust had disappeared and the sled runners dug twelve to fourteen inches into the snow. It was tough sledding except in the foot paths about the village.

Father Rooney heaved his great bulk from a comfortable position in the komatik and strode up to the porch.

"Merry Christmas, Tom!"

He smiled and shook the officer's hand firmly. These two were long time friends. Twenty years ago they had joined the Ranger force together. Their paths had separated and now the one who had left to become a priest was back in his former home with the folks he had once helped and protected in quite another way.

Tom grasped his friend's hand. "Merry Christmas, Jim, come in and have a drink."

"Well, just a little spirit, Tom. Marie and the children aren't coming until this evening. I really came because I thought that from Marie's talk about you and your prisoner, you could stand a little companionship this Christmas day. Two fellows like you two here are really two fellows apart."

The priest inclined his head a trifle and lifted an eyebrow in looking at his friend.

Jim stayed a while, visiting the prisoner and chatting the afternoon away with Tom. He left and held afternoon mass in the village, then returned sometime past three. He has just returned and was making himself comfortable with his friend again when the faint barking of dogs brought them both to their feet. They moved out of the building together and watched the distant komatik and team. The corporal put his glasses on them.

"It's Louie, all right." He turned to the priest and grinned. "Christmas for me tonight! Marie and the kids had their presents this morning, but it'll be Christmas all over again for them when they show them to me."

The priest smiled warmly. Tom did have a big heart. Good thoughts flooded his mind about him. "The next time I hear Tom complain will be the first time," he thought.

They watched the party moving closer. The barking was becoming more distinct. It sounded more like dogs now and less like geese.

They were watching when the team and the komatik disappeared. In an instant there were no dogs, no sled, no driver, no nothing!

For a moment neither man moved. What passed as hours were only seconds. Tom ran first. He ran and shouted.

"Rope! Get rope! Hurry!"

He shouted to no one. On Christmas afternoon after mass everyone was inside. Families were together today. Every family about the Bight was opening gifts or eating Christmas dinner or swapping yarns at this very moment.

Father Rooney crossed himself. "Go, Tom, I'll get rope!" He ran for the church.

Tom ran out on what had been ice. It was only slob now. Yesterday morning it had been crusty, solid, snow-ice. Today it was slob and slush. He slipped once or twice and fell, picked himself up and went on. Five minutes from shore he saw it. A great wide swatch of salt slush. Deep sled tracks led up to it from the west. The marks of struggling dogs, their nail prints clear, ripped the slob at the edge on the other side. They had struggled to gain safety on the broken ice and failed. Slush covered all but a narrow strip of green water in the centre now. The corporal dropped to his knees and crawled forward, shouting. He shouted to his family, calling their names, names *he* had always called them. He shouted to God! There was no answer; and no sign anywhere over the slob ice of the harbour that he had been heard.

Tears dropped in the salty mush as the corporal inched ahead. The whole wide sheet was settling with his weight now, settling slowly, like a cushion. There now! In the small bit of open water he spotted something, something blue. Crawling along, sinking lower, with water now up to his elbows and covering his legs, he reached out, almost grasping something that was left. Stretching more, across the whole gap now, his fingers touched and then squeezed.

It was a moment before he began to inch backward slowly, sobbing, toward safety. The water almost covered him and he tried to stand, slipped and then thrust himself backward with a mighty push of his feet as the slob ice gave way and the powerful hands of

Father Rooney grasped his collar, pulling him from death and his family.

Before long, people began to gather cautiously about. No one talked as they stood and watched the sobbing corporal, shivering in his wet uniform. In his hands he clutched a little blue mitt with a red stain.

Part III

If It's Good For a Scoff...

Animals and People

Our views of wild things are founded on experience. If it is our custom to use fish we catch or animals we kill only for food or for monetary gain, we think of wildlife much differently than one who has never shared such experiences. These five stories are about a people and their views toward wild things you may not always feel kindly toward. Nevertheless, they are real. In this part we mention Tom Bergerud, Jack Saunders, Steve Hall, Selby Moss, Uncle Bren Tilley, Bob Folker, Clarence Elms, Gordie Butt, Ron Hounsell, Art Taylor, Corporal Hogan, Magistrate White, Dave Pike, Eldon Pace, Constable Porter and Constable Haddad, Dr. Bob Dove, Jack Nichols, Ron Callahan and Art Butt. All other names of characters are fictitious.

Rangifer

Perhaps because I had learned much about nature from my father and my grandfather, it was natural for me to visit older Newfoundlanders who had spent much of their lives 'in the country.' I also learned from these men and I owe much to them today. Years later, in central Africa, my superior in the Food and Agricultural Organization of the United Nations suggested the same approach.

"Ask the old men of the villages," he said. "You'll learn more than you will through field research in the little time you have. Do the field work, certainly, but don't neglect the old people, the hunters and the village elders and the shamans. Run everything they tell you through that fanning mill between your ears and you could be rewarded beyond your dreams."

He really didn't have to tell me of the potential value of such an approach. I'd begun to learn it as a boy with 'Rip,' my grandfather, and I'd honed my listening abilities and already improved my fanning mill process somewhat in Newfoundland.

Perhaps more important than the natural history information learned is the understanding one gains of people's attitudes along with something of the sources of those attitudes. For caribou there were feelings of the lingering dream of an abundance—somewhere—that would surely return; of a longing for the glory days of past caribou hunting to return; of competition between humans and wolves, always exaggerated since wolves were never plentiful and were extinct by 1911; days, of course, that might not return.

I also knew a man who killed the last of the caribou that existed then on the White Bay Downs.

"Rangifer" is a story about Newfoundland caribou and about people's attitudes, their knowledge and sometimes their misinterpretations of what they observed. At the time this story was written, the cause of the great calf losses and the caribou decline were still a mystery. Soon after, however, a team lead by Tom Bergerud determined that a complex of synergistic relations among lynx, a normal bacterium of the mouth and head sinuses of lynx, the protective behaviour of female caribou, and the natural fluctuations of the introduced snowshoe hare combined to cause their deaths. Lynx would attack caribou calves when hare densities were low, bite the calf, introducing the bacterium and then be driven off by the adult female caribou. The calf would perish.

Let us consider the story of "Rangifer," written in 1956, before the mystery was unravelled, and listen to a few of the people who knew the caribou then.

❧

Each April there is one day in the northern forests unmistakably different from all the days before. It is that day when the fading winter draughts are first joined by the warmer gusts that herald the return of spring.

This one day always arrives during a period of bright, sunny daylight, glistening, ice-covered snow, and cloudless, frosty darkness. It is a period of orientation for all mammal life and all bird life. This day signifies the end of the cold, still, heavy days of winter and the beginning of the revival of life.

There had been a week of bright, sunny, cold days in this April 1960. The woodland was crusted, even in the most dense cover—crusted so firmly the sharp-hoofed moose could tread without breaking through. At night the frost-crystals would settle to the solid surface of the land and forest, so that at each sunrise the world of white was softly blanketed with a new, clean smoothness, and the animals that moved during the early morning hours left their almost invisible prints behind them.

On the high, barren, snow-blown slopes of Mount St. Gregory the blue snow-ice glistened in the sunlight. In some places it reflected starlight, and the moon's rays danced crazily from it slanting, uneven ridges. During the early darkness of these days an accompanying wonderment of skylight, the dancing curtains, framed this mountain with wavering sheets of brightness meeting at the top, the centre of all the sparkling universe, in a rounded ball of glistening red and yellow.

On the plateau itself, stretching along North Arm on the south, bordering the evergreen forest on the east and the Trout River Ponds to the north, ice covered the slopes below the naked ridge-tops and above the snow-crusted flats of the valleys. In these valleys, the valleys of Liverpool and Crabbs Brook, only trickles of water moved, for the frost had eaten the moisture this winter and pushed to the base rock over all the plateau and the mountain. It was a time of quiet life, past the dreaded winter's deadness and yet too early for the gushers of water to be brought by the coming spring.

At this time of the year the Gregory caribou herd always became restless. Within weeks, now, the does must be on their fawning grounds, many miles from this wind-swept mountain country. For centuries the round-hoofed, grey-coated spring animals had moved down the rocky cliffs from the plateau to the forest and travelled north across the Governors Pond woodland lichen country, through the timber, and on to the great chain of hills leading north on the peninsula. There, the does made their way to the yellow bogs and gave birth while the stags wandered about singly or in small companies, living slowly, moving little, putting on fat.

The caribou had always lived on the Gregory Plateau for part of the year. They moved onto the highland area at the first snowfall of autumn and ate the lichens on the great mountain slopes and the slopes overlooking Chimney Cove, the Gregory River and the Trout River ponds. In stormy weather they moved into the valleys of the brooks and fed on the tree lichens that grew in abundance from the spruce. If the storms were prolonged and the winds westerly, the animals sometimes moved into the forest below the great rock cliff boarders of the plateau. This country was rich in lichens both on the ground and on the spruce and larch trees, present in park-like stands over the knolls to the greater valley. Then, sometime in late April, the animals trekked north, away from the plateau to the northern hills. It was on this trek and in those hills that they sometimes mingled with other herds of caribou from the Humber Valley, the Topsail barrens, and Hinds plains. Some years, the Gregory herd would be increased by wanderers from other herds and some years it would be decreased when a few of its own body would stray to other groups and move away to a different country. These stragglers were often young, anxious, adventurous stags in search of does.

It was 10 April 1960 when Rangifer felt the first warm draughts, mixed with the clinging cold of the waning winter. During the past few days he had been feeding upon tree lichen in the valley of Crabbs Brook. All his life he had fed on the lichens hanging from the slow growing spruce and fir in this valley. He liked both the black lichens and the yellow-green ones. They were good for him during the late winter and early spring and he sough them out instinctively.

This day, Rangifer moved slowly over the blue ice, his broad, round hoofs making sure of safe footing on the glazed and glassy surface. He headed for the lichen stands; ground cover in the area of dense heath, which stayed blown clear most years because of its position on the hanging western abutments of Mount St. Gregory. Reflected from the blue surface, the sun's heat made the densely coated animal slacken his pace and sometimes pause. He passed the boulder garden about the peak, still stopping occasionally, and settled after a moment's hesitation on a protected spot at the end of a small yellow marsh. He was no longer interested in his destination and he lay facing the breezes, his front legs tucked in under him. The tops of the yellowed old-year grass-like bulrush waved from the light, unsettled snow cover, outlining the shape of the marsh he was in.

The woodland caribou lives alone with his kind apart from other mammal life. His home is sometimes wind-swept, rock-spotted and barren, or it may be protected, level, parkland cover. The caribou lives by movement—wild and independent. His movements are directed by weather and by his changing seasonal requirements for food that grow in particular sites.

The movement from behind the boulder was slight. The man stepped into the open and stood motionless. Rangifer, facing away into the wind, did not move. His senses told him nothing of what might be behind. He lived facing the wind, depending on his sense of smell to keep him from danger.

Rangifer heard the shot and trembled more from the impact of the bullet than from fright. Slowly he worked his legs under him to withstand his body's weight and pushed himself up, hind quarters first. Turning, he saw the man, blurred to him, fifty yards away. The man was standing quietly, watching his target. There was, he knew, no need to fire again. The caribou moved slowly towards the danger as if trying to distinguish this new strangeness. Closer, slowly closer, his great bulk moved. He coughed and bright red blood spattered the snow-sheet before him. Close enough now to detect the odour, even against the wind, Rangifer gradually settled down to rest. This was the end of Rangifer's life, which has begun almost four years before.

Rangifer was born on 24 May 1956. His mother, Tarandus, had chosen the edge of an open bog near a tiny clump of black spruce growing from a dry, four-inch mat of yellow-grey lichens. She had carried him for two hundred and twenty-seven days from the day of conception the preceding October.

He was a perfect offspring and stood shakily to feed four hours after birth. Tarandus had cleansed him dry right after birth. He was a light reddish-brown, almost tan, with a dark brown-black muzzle. All little caribou look the same, but each is quite special to the mother animal.

The first day Tarandus stayed with her offspring except for quick, casual trips of a few yards for water and green food. Towards the evening of the second day she nuzzled him to accompany her about the open marsh. They moved slowly northward towards the great grassy marshes at the headwaters of Crabbs Brook valley two miles away. At times Rangifer would frisk ahead of his mother as she stopped to feed. Often he nursed hungrily. Soon his mother would feel the energy drain and feed more herself.

By dark they were standing alone on a tiny peninsula stretching into a shallow steady in the brook. Here they lay down. Twice during the night they moved together about the marsh for an hour or more as Tarandus fed. For the rest of the night they slept, and daylight found them standing in the great marsh, Tarandus feeding upon the tender green shoots of early spring while Rangifer nursed.

It was long after daylight when Rangifer detected the presence of other caribou. Tarandus had known—had expected them to be here on this day, at this time. She had lived for seven years now and for the past five years she had produced young on the same fawning ground. She had moved here instinctively the first year immediately after the birth. The other does and their fawns were here then and they had always been here since. This year's lapse of time, staying alone with her offspring, was unusual. Sometimes a few days would elapse before they would all be together but gather they must, and did.

One day, eons of time before Tarandus, a group of twenty doe caribou had gathered together with their helpless fawns by sheer accident, having fought off three wolves. Throughout the years other events like this had occurred and the protective habit persisted. Now there are no wolves and few bears here, but the pattern remains, perhaps for future needs.

There were fifteen other does and nine fawns on the great yellow marsh five days later. The fawns were all light brown with dark muzzles. The does were a shabby grey-white in their winter's garment. After the early morning feeding, the does would gradually bed down to cud while their offspring slept or rested beside them. Soon after noon, the first doe would stand and begin to graze. By mid-afternoon all the herd would be feeding, the fawns frisking about the mothers and the barren does. These dry does took considerable interest in all the offspring of the herd.

Rangifer played all afternoon with the other fawns, feeding at intervals. If another fawn tried to nurse with Rangifer, he balked at this attempt at sharing so that the visitor would usually stand at a safe distance and watch after a few short challenges from Rangifer. If the other fawn persisted, the victimized cow would strike at the intruder with forefeet or charge threateningly.

One day, when Rangifer was four weeks old, a nearby female fawn became sick. Instead of playing actively, she held her head to one side, staggered when trying to stand and refused nourishment. Her condition became worse the next day, and on the third day a great hole appeared in the side of her neck. White, pasty fluid drained from the opening. The fawn could no longer stand after the hole appeared and the doe seldom moved more than twenty or thirty feet away. The emaciated animal died where she lay. For several days the mother remained nearby until one day she moved out among the other animals, mothering fawns that stood alone. She continued to travel with the group until it began to disintegrate in early July. After the death of this first fawn, many others fell ill. Only Rangifer and one other were spared. By early July, five of the original ten had died. The other three, which were also afflicted, had recovered. Some of the illnesses had come as a result of an attack by lynx. Where the sharp canine teeth had penetrated, bacteria entered the blood stream of the hapless calves. Yet cases of the sickness in some remain a mystery to man even today.

Throughout the summer months, Rangifer often saw one or more of his early playmates. At times several caribou would be together and sometimes Rangifer and Tarandus would be alone for days. He fed considerably on grasses and sedges after the first of July and by September he spent as much time grazing and browsing as his mother did, though he still nursed when Tarandus let him.

September found the whole caribou herd on the great North Arm barrens. There were four small groups totalling thirty-five animals. Rangifer and Tarandus were with seven other caribou. One great stag dominated the group and although he never chased Rangifer he often threatened the medium-sized stag and the small yearling stag, known to man as a pricket. Three old does and a yearling pricket doe were also in the group. Rangifer paid little attention to this gathering of animals, though he felt less closely attached to this mother than he had during the warm weeks of the past summer.

Within this harem unit no one challenged the great stag's supremacy, but once, in mid-September, a stag from another group came very close. The great stag moved towards the intruder, head down, slowly waving from side to side. The intruding stag, at least as big as the Great One, met the challenge and the two placed their antlers together. Suddenly they tensed, muscles rippling and bulging. Each strained to shove the other backwards. The great stag slowly inched ahead as the intruder weakened. Then in an instant the intruder was pushed back and stumbled. As his side struck the ground with a thud, he struggled away from the victor. The great stag stood menacingly above, staring and moving his head but making no attempt this time to gore the helpless, defeated animal. Thoroughly beaten, the intruder made his way toward the group from which he had come.

The does and prickets in Rangifer's group had watched the battle intently. The whole affair took about three minutes, yet the defeat was complete and the stags so near exhaustion that the Great One gasped for breath, his sides swelling and shrinking deeply for minutes after. This was Rangifer's first experience of fighting among his own kind. He would live to see several more battles and to take part himself.

On 1 October the four groups joined on the eastern end of the North Arm barrens, not far from the tinkling headwaters of Liverpool Brook. For four days the largest of the stags asserted their supremacy by chasing younger males and occasionally challenging each other. There were only two exceptionally large stags, the Great One and the animal he had already defeated, but three others were large enough to assert themselves successfully, so that the herd had five master stags.

The herd remained as one unit, except for the loss of does after conception, for three weeks. Master stags battled furiously on occasion, but the younger males moved away from slight, intimidating advances made by the older ones. Sometimes an old stag like the Great One would stand bush-gazing, motionless for an hour or more, staring in one direction, his neck bent slightly downwards.

On 11 October the first mating occurred. Tarandus had reached her time and the Great One sought her out. Two other does also conceived on this day and mating continued until the last doe was bred on 17 October.

Three days after Tarandus had conceived she moved away, followed by Rangifer. The two other does that had conceived at the same time as Tarandus also left. After each female mated the group shrank, until by 18 October only the yearlings, stags and barren does remained.

Slowly the group disintegrated and a ragged exodus began as the animals moved along the barrens towards the head waters in the brook valleys. Here in the wide basin of the head of Crabbs Brook was the pass in the hills, no longer used by the animals. At one time great numbers of caribou filed between these hills, where the settlers from Trout River met the animals, and killed them. Today the deer stayed in the valleys or moved aimlessly back across the barrens.

During the post-breeding restlessness, four hunters climbed the bluffs from North Arm and searched the barrens for ptarmigan and hare. They knew the Gregory Plateau well and had hunted here all their lives. Hunting without dogs, they killed a great many ptarmigan and a few hares, and each man killed a caribou, though for over twenty years caribou shooting had been prohibited here.

After a long mid-winter spent in the great lowland country about Governors Pond, on the barrens and on Mount St. Gregory, the month of March found the caribou moving aimlessly once again over the snow-crust. March also brought the settlers up from Chimney Cove to kill their annual caribou. There were six families living in Chimney Cove now and ten men represented these families on the slopes of the windswept mountain. They killed ten caribou, grouped as they stood. Twenty-one animals remained on the plateau, nineteen fewer than there had been after fawning a year before.

Old men can also tell us a part of the story, though they sometimes err in their beliefs of what exists today.

"We used to kill caribou and taste the wolf on 'em. They was run ragged over from the tablelands, down across the pond, up the gulch and over to the mountain and back again. Two, three times they'd go maybe, but the wolf 'ud get the deer every time.

"I know. I seen 'em do it. Why, one morning I was goin' down the ice hopin' to get a deer at the head of the gulch or in the pass when I come across the tracks. They was blood there then, where the wolf was nippin' the hocks of the deer. They was headed east up to the tablelands. Then just after I passed the tracks I heard something comin' and sure 'nuff back a me and a-comin' down off the Table Mountain was a deer and on his heels was the wolf! They was too far to shoot so after they'd gone up the west side slippin' and slidin' I went back a couple of hundred yards and waited.

"Well sir, I packed out two quarters and the hide on me hand sled but never went back after the rest. You could taste the wolf on 'em easy enough!

"Nowadays the deer has gone altogether. Warn't more'n twenty year past I killed the last 'un right out there on the pond ice. There ain't no more now. Least, I never seen none the past twenty year and I don't believe anyone else has either. Course, could be the deer don't use this side of Crow Head no more and maybe if they's still there they stays in one place.

"We used to depend on deer here all right. Every spring in March month we'd git deer, all we wanted right handy. Some fellers went down the coast and up. I know old Jobie used to go in the country from Sally's Cove with komatik and team and he'd bring out six, seven deer to once. Sometimes them fellas 'ud go in and kill the deer in early winter then go back in March and bring 'em out. Sometimes they'd run into more deer on the way fer the meat and leave the cached meat where't lay. Fergit altogether 'cause it was easier killin' again.

"Times was once when some of the boys down the coast used to go in and kill twenty, thirty deer just fer a fry of tongues.

"The deer are all gone now, boy! They don't come 'round here no more. All moved back into the country. Must be thousands back in the country, though. Least, there used to be thousands right down here. Why, I seen deer right there next to my barn in the spring of the year. They was all over the Table Mountain and down Indian Head and up Crow Head.

"No more wolves, neither. Fact is I killed the last wolf right there on the river back of the mill about forty, fifty years ago. Must of been about 1910 or thereabouts. Always figgered there must be lots of wolves, but we never seen one after that."

Rangifer was one year old in June 1957. Fleet afoot, deep chested and strong, the yearling caribou was the animal most sought after by meat hunters in years past. The first antler growth was apparent now. Velvet spikes and brow stood from the bony knobs on Rangifer's head.

No longer with his mother, who had long since deserted him to calve, Rangifer roamed with a large stag, the Great One, over the plateau and the flat Governors Pond wood and lichen country. Now, after the winter's diet of tree lichens and ground lichens, the caribou fed lavishly on the green shoots of wild grasses, sedges and rushes. When the ice covered their feeding grounds on the heights, the caribou had moved to the valley and were forced to dig through many feet of snow to obtain their lichen diet. They fed on the buds and bark of larch and from the hanging festoons of tree lichens on the larch and spruce, when available. Now they would vary their diet through the summer and fall, adding many items to it. In all, the deer would feed upon forty or more species of fungi, lichens and herbaceous and woody plants through the year.

One morning, as Rangifer lay on a rock outcrop overlooking a small pond, he noticed a movement strange to him. Turning, he watched the Great One, who lay nearby, looking for a sign he might follow. The Great One saw the movement too but paid it little heed. He had often watched the moose feeding during the summers past.

The moose fed on grasses and rushes at the edge of the pond. He too was taking on a new diet from his winter's woody twigs. The greens in the marshes would be added to as the summer progressed. Later he would feed on aquatic plants and all through the summer he would seek out the young leaves of birch and willow.

As the huge beast moved about the edge of the pond close to Rangifer, the pricket stag grew excited. The moose was a large bull. Its velveted antlers were still small but the bulk of the animal more than doubled Rangifer's. In a short while the moose was abreast of the young deer and, catching scent of another animal, it turned. From twenty feet they watched each other. Rangifer lay with his front legs under him, bent at the knees. His hind legs were drawn up close so that with only a slight roll of his weight they would be under him and he would be bounding away, head and tail held high. But the pricket stag was curious too, so he lay watching, smelling, listening intently, ready to move but waiting for a sign from the moose or the great stag. No sign was given. After a moment's examination of the smaller animal, the moose continued his feeding, moving steadily along the pond's edge. Rangifer watched until the animal drifted into cover minutes after.

❧

Now a biologist studies the caribou—too late.

"I first saw the animals from the helicopter in July. We set up camp and worked over the herd for sex and age ratios for three weeks. The range is adequate and I think the herd could continue as it is or maybe increase with protection, barring heavy losses from this crazy disease we're trying to fathom.

"We caught two men from a woods camp with two animals which they claimed to have killed for camp meat. This is what the mining camp foreman used to do before the herd was reduced, I guess. The men were charged, found guilty and let off with suspended sentences. This isn't good enough and as far as I'm concerned, the animals are finished now. They are too far removed from people to create any political interest and I've been ordered to work on the big interior herds and those small ones closer to town."

❧

Rangifer moved with the Great One even after the large animal turned on him several times during September. During this month they sought out Tarandus and her spring fawn and another doe and her fawn. These does were with the Great One in his harem of past years, for the Great One was Rangifer's father and the father of all Tarandus' offsprings.

All the stags now wore their clean, white neck manes over swollen muscles. Their contrasting white and brown separated them from the duller grey-brown does—drab besides the noble looking male animals. This year, Rangifer was chased often, not only by the Great One but by the other larger stags.

The breeding took place as always, and after the month's activity Rangifer moved about with the Great One again. They were together all winter and throughout the month of March when the Chimney Cove hunters returned and took seven of the remaining animals, as many as had been born that year.

There had been no sickness last spring, but nine does had been killed and before the fawning season of 1958 only nineteen caribou remained in the Gregory herd.

❧

What is the attitude of the woods contractor who, perhaps unknowingly, has the power to maintain this herd and others like it?

"When we first opened the road into Taylors Brook, there were hundreds of caribou all around the camps. We killed one each during the season in 1949 and again in 1950. Then in 1951 we had to move up to the Neds Steady Crossing and were lucky enough to get a few. The next year no caribou crossed there at all. They just went.

"Oh, they're still in the valley, all right. They moves down on the Great Northern Peninsula, you know. Thousands of them down there. I've heard tell of men seein' herds of two, three hundred when they were in furrin' back of Silver Mountain.

"Now we moved up here by Governors Pond and I'm dammed if there ain't a whack of deer right behind us on that plateau there. Why. last year two of the boys went up there and killed two in the summer. Course they got caught but it was only an accident that the warden happened along and then they got off anyway.

"Now we got this here fawn we picked up. Took six of us to corner him. Boy, could he run! But we got 'im and we're feeding him milk. Boys sure like him around the camp, you know. Makes a great pet.

"What's that, cook? What? Where is he? What's the matter with him? Dead? Well' I'll be damned! Look here, the damned deer died on us."

Five fawns had been born this season and one was caught and carried away by woodsmen. Then in the fall hunters from the woods camp came onto the plateau again. The contractor led his men to the breeding herd and they killed twelve deer. Tarandus and her last fawn were killed.

Rangifer roamed the country with the Great One during the winter. They no longer travelled down into the flat Governors Pond lichen country.

In January there was a great storm. The caribou grew restless and milled about for two days in the blizzard. On the third day, the Great One disappeared as he walked beside Rangifer. He had stumbled over the ledge and fallen into North Arm. This left ten deer to perpetuate the herd.

When spring came once more to the tiny group of deer, two fawns were born. One doe, a barren animal, was without antlers, but the does with fawns had carried their antlers until the fawns were dropped. A fourth doe had borne no fawn because she was sickly. The four does were all that was left of the once great fawning herd that had in past years travelled fifty miles or more to the endless grassy leads on the western end of the Great Northern Peninsula to drop their young.

As they had always done, the does kept with their fawns throughout the summer. They watched a female bear and her cubs feeding on old-year berries and new-year grasses. They knew where the geese nested and reared their young and they watched the white-headed eagles soar over the bluffs along the Gulf of St. Lawrence.

Frisking over the marshes like windblown leaves, the caribou fawns lived their young lives as hundreds of others had done in this herd before them, and just as Rangifer had done. Once, in late summer, Rangifer and the barren doe, who were travelling together, watched a fox catch a moulting duck along the edge of a marshy pond. Life was complete in the deer world for those who remained, even to the nose bots which had so pestered Rangifer since his first year. There was no warning to the individual caribou that the end was near. The fawns of this spring did not know they were the last.

Besides Rangifer, two other stags remained. One was too aged, the other too weak to stand against the powerful thrusts of the beautiful young stag. In October, Rangifer fought and defeated them both. Rangifer was master of the herd, a group of twelve, including two male fawns.

The mating season came upon them. Rangifer mated two does. Another doe, the one that had been ill, now was sickly and thin, so she took no part in the breeding activities. Rangifer was the master stag when only three years and four months old.

Soon after the rut and breeding was finished, the hunters came from the woods camp. The contractor and his men shot and killed eleven caribou, including the emaciated doe, which was left along with the aged stag to rot on the mountain slopes.

Beoth

One cold February evening in 1957, Jack Saunders, a biologist friend, and I were returning to our truck parked near the bridge at Harriman's Brook Crossing. We had snowshoed several miles across the Cormack burn towards Adies River and back that day, looking for lynx tracks. Occasionally we had followed one for a half-mile or so. Now the sun was dropping swiftly and only frail rays of light showed above the White Hills as we crossed a frozen pond. Suddenly we both stopped our shuffling gait. Each of us had seen the tracks ahead at the same time and each of us moved up to them, bent down, examining them closely. One set of tracks crossed the crusted snow that covered the ice, very large tracks from a member of the dog family. But there were no dogs here. Both of us knew that no family owning a dog lived within fifteen miles of where we stood and the dog that family owned, even though it was large, made a track only half the size of this one. There were simply no dogs in all the Humber District that could have made such a track!

Neither of us spoke. We did not stand and look at each other and there was no need to say anything. There were no wolves in Newfoundland.

Once there had been wolves. They probably moved with the deer, Rangifer and his kind, from the Ungava thousands of years ago. The Beothuks knew them well and may have tamed a pup now and then. But by 1911 few, if any, were left. Never abundant, they finally succumbed to the Europeans' fear of them after nearly 400 years. Still, here on this sub zero evening we stood looking at the print of a wolf. Or, was it?

That night I dreamed of Beoth.

❧

It was the wind that spoke. At first the voice was distant, unclear. The words were muffled as if the frosted branches of the dense fir forest were blotting out what I strained to hear. I moved outside my tent and stood over the staccato fire that boiled the kettle and listened. Perhaps I had been wrong and had heard no voice at all. No, the murmur was there, tremulous, whispering, now stronger, now fading. If only the branches did not crack and rattle so! There now, a word spoken clearly. It came not only from windward but from all the forest. 'Wolf.' Certainly it was meant for me.

Many times during the past few winters I had heard a wolf from the north or from the south or east or west. I had myself seen a track, though it certainly could not have been, for wolves no longer exist in Newfoundland. Yet today again I saw the track, bold, in fresh snow atop the crust, and I followed it. Through stunted fir, across marshes, out of my way I followed it, determined to see, to find the source of the pads upon the snow.

In mid-afternoon I found the kill. A moose calf, emaciated from some sickness or abnormality, had this January day fallen victim, perhaps for the good of its kind. The throat was torn and the beast's eyes bulged in death, the terror of the attack increased by the presence of the predator so many years extinct.

Extinct? How could this be? I left the animal, still warm with clotted blood frosting over the portions from which great jaws had torn flesh, and followed until dark overcame me in this small valley among the Hobblies. I made camp under the firs, though the tracks continued.

Now the wind whispered clearly, 'Wolf—wolf—wolf.' I felt no fear, but I could not speak, nor did I feel the need. Alone, I stood attentive to the wind.

❧

Cold light shone one night many years ago on the barren mountain you know as Soldiers Hill. Mist rose as clouds from ponds dotting the sloping plateau toward the east, then moved slowly, white billows, soldiers of the moon god. Effortlessly to and fro about the treeless plains they move.

In the valleys below the slopes no light shone. The moon was not high enough in its majesty to penetrate all this living world, and dead.

On the mountainside dotted with boulders gleaming from cold crystals, once molten, a life lay quiet, motionless as the rocks themselves. This was Beoth, wolf-son of Lupus. Somewhere in the vastness of the night Lupus was cutting and tearing the shank of a caribou killed during the early morning of that same day. She would bring the shank to her offspring.

Beoth sat up. He had waited long, and impatience is strong in the young. As he sat up, there suddenly lay before him a great black wolf, much larger that Beoth or Lupus or any other. Beoth stood and, as he did so, the black wolf grew larger. Quickly Beoth jumped behind a boulder. The black wolf appeared beside him, covering, blotting out, the stone of refuge.

Beoth ran down the slope, thunder beating within his ears. The black wolf matched his leaps, always beside him. Suddenly, into the darkened vale the tormentor was gone. Beoth, alone again, learned then that his world was darkness. To the wolf, light is fear, night is peace. Beoth waited for his mother.

Beoth grew until he was the largest of the remaining wolves, those that had not fallen prey to traps of steel, snares of wire or lead from guns. With his mother and a wolf family from far to the north, he hunted the caribou, following the animals to their breeding grounds, their wintering yards, north in the late winter with the great migration and back again in the fall. On the spring calving grounds the wolves fared best. Though the does gathered together with their fawns for protection, there was seldom need to attack the healthy. There were often sick ones or weak ones the herd would be better off without. Indeed, the wolves' attacks saved many caribou lives, because sickness could not spread when the ill were removed from the living group at the first sign of weakness.

So too, many years before, the wolf had been friend to the Indian for whom Beoth was named. Each creature feared the other, each one's life depended upon the caribou. The wolf lived on the sick, the old, the emaciated—the Indian upon the fat, the strong, the healthy. Though each feared the other, the Indian respected *Moisamadrook,* the wolf, for his strength, his cunning, his fearlessness in darkness. *Moisamadrook,* the wolf, respected the Indian for his dead falls, his snares of caribou thong and his arrows. But the Indian killed few wolves. Other furs were more lasting, like the seal and the otter. Some were more beautiful, like the marten and ermine. Most were easier to take, especially the beaver.

In turn, the wolf avoided the red man except during the fall and spring hunts when the Indian killed many caribou; more than he could use, leaving carcasses for *Moisamadrook*.

But now, in the time of Beoth, the Indian, friend of the wolf and of all the wild, was gone, destroyed by the scourge that now threatened Beoth and Lupus and all the breed. A scourge of death.

❧

The wind increased. Boughs snapped around me. For a moment the voice was gone. I felt despair, yet my heart beat wildly, as I thought of the track, and a vision of what must surely come filled my mind. The gust subsided, leaving branches hanging, swaying loosely in a gentle night.

I looked down at the fire, though I was warm. Wood had been added. My only need had been cared for. I was free to listen to the wind.

Again, as before, the murmur began, faintly distant, fading, then clearing, until the whisper broke from all around me - 'Wolf.'

❧

Beoth, the great grey wolf, grew and hunted and mated. He played with his pups and brought food for them to eat. Though his own father had been killed before his birth, Beoth from the first helped care for his offspring. Each year the white man destroyed many wolves and fewer and fewer were left to breed. Only in the interior wilderness were wolves to be found, and even here the white and the Micmac doggedly hunted, trapped and killed.

So it was that within a year from their birth the pups were destroyed. Beoth's mate was dead and of the pack only Beoth and Lupus remained. Bounty killers had selfishly persevered until the very source was gone.

Now Beoth and Lupus roamed together—Lupus, the old mother, dependent upon her strong offspring. Though her cunning guided the hunt, it was Beoth who killed. Though her cunning often saved their lives, it was Beoth who destroyed the snares and sprang the traps.

The two no longer killed caribou unless an unfortunate crippled or sick animal wandered near. The old weakened wolf was no longer able to follow the herds. They fed on hare or roosting ptarmigan, depending upon their wits to capture them.

Still, when the caribou began their trek the two wolves followed for a time, hoping, yet not daring to attack. They chanced on a caribou wounded by a hunter and relieved their gnawing hunger.

Beoth lay resting on the bare side hill watching Lupus feed below him in the valley. The doe caribou had been fat and dry—choice meat after a diet of hare and partridge. The scent of man filled his nostrils, making them flare as he breathed out to weaken the poisoned air. He could not warn Lupus. The wolf must not howl in the presence of man, as an enemy. Lupus would certainly scent the danger in time.

Beoth stood motionless, the hair at his back and neck rigid, low growls curling from the depths of his giant body. Lupus, busy with her meal, was eating steadily with her poor teeth and tired jaws. Lupus was shot and killed.

Alone, Beoth began a great journey. Across lands unknown to him he trod, silent as death itself, the one last member of his breed. Across frozen lakes, over mountains and valleys, through marsh and forests—winter, spring, summer, fall—Beoth walked. No man would kill this great grey wolf. None could approach him. He carried all the cunning, intelligence and dignity of his breed.

Mating seasons came and passed. In the cold, pale light of the moon, Beoth lifted voice to all his kind, yet found no mate.

He wandered the land—and back—east to west, north to south—Doctors Hills, Lewis Hills, Blue Hills of Coteau, Lobster House, Mounts Peyton, Sylvester and Sykes. He roamed, pausing to kill, to eat, to live.

Somewhere, some time, death came to Beoth.

Beoth, the grey wolf ghost, roams today over the same plateau, valley and hill, through the same forests, stunted fir and barren. His tracks are seen, and sometimes in the pale, cold light Beoth, too, is seen.

Death to the wolf is to roam and kill, somewhere in a living land. Beoth, the last, roams his land and that of all his kind. The land belongs to Beoth and to the Beothuk.

What are the great rocks gleaming beneath the moon and stars? Boulders, you say, left from glaciers, relics, remnants of the past? Ah, no, they are markers. Count them—markers for all the wolves, the Indians, whose very breath you have stolen. Beoth paces now among them, on Mount St. Gregory, Blue Hills of Couteau and Soldiers Hill.

There is no need to travel further. You may return. Beoth cannot be pursued. By good fortune only, you may see the grey wolf ghost, and only by the full moon's light.

❧

Again the wind shatters the frozen branches above me. This time the flame flickers and suddenly rises to greater brightness. I am restless and walk around my camp, beyond the wavering light of the flames. Tracks all about me, all around the camp, approaching the edge of the early glow of the flame. Beoth, the grey wolf ghost. Was it the wind that spoke?

Now the flame is gone, dying to its natural embers as if no wood had been added. The wind has died and no breeze stirs as I move slowly towards my tent to rest.

Excerpts from Pearl's Letters Home

Dear Folks...

July, 1955

Well, I thought, today I can settle down to routine. It was Monday. I did my laundry with my gas washing machine and also baked bread. Just as I was running the last pair of pants through the wringer, a knock cane at the door. It was a business associate and friend of Don's. They had left St. John's a week ago and were now headed back, but they stayed for dinner and ate steak. They had been spending time putting up mist nets in various places to catch birds for banding and this was the interesting part about their visit. They put a mist net up in the bushes back of the house and netted a male and female purple finch and a yellow-bellied flycatcher. I was thrilled to see these birds so close; in fact, I held the male purple finch in my hand. He was lovely. It was the first time I had ever seen any banding operations.

Our visitors were headed for Gales Bottom to do some more netting and banding and I'll be darned if Don didn't go with them! Well, he was here long enough for me to wash his clothes anyway. It was gone Thursday, back Sunday. Now it's gone Monday, back Thursday.

Before they left, the climax of the day. The lynx we've talked so much about arrived. She had been shipped by boat from Hawks Bay on Friday and Steve picked her up at Corner Brook today. Poor thing, no food or water, and now she has to be subjected to the cage on our lawn. Yes, it's a she. And her name? Why, "Wiley Cat," of course. You non-Pogo fans many not recognize this name. She looks much like an ordinary tiger house cat, only about four times bigger. Even so, Don says she's a small animal. Short stubby tail and two-inch tufts on her ears. She looks quite petable until you take a look at her claws. Very frightened, she cowers in the farthest corner and growls at any movement or noise. We spent $2.50 on a live chicken for Wiley Cat, hoping she would eat it. When I went to bed at eleven o'clock the chicken was still very much alive, but the lynx was eating a piece of liver we had given her.

The next day found the chicken still alive. Our worry now is that the lynx won't eat in captivity. We certainly hope she will and will do everything possible to keep her healthy. We've gained a lynx but lost our privacy. There were eight kids in the yard this morning, but the men are putting up another fence around the cages to keep people away from the animals. Cars are stopping out front to gaze.

As we eat at the kitchen table we can look out at our private zoo. The woods in back of the house is our bird paradise and we feel we are very, very fortunate.

September, 1955

Now who in the ever lovin' blue-eyed world would have thought that Don would be out catching poachers? Poaching is done openly up here. Moose meat, illegally shot, is even sold door-to-door in Corner Brook. A few miles down the road a couple of weeks ago a beautiful big bull was shot and then abandoned in fear. It seems to be one of those situations that just can't be managed. The Mounties are far too busy with other work and there is a lot of woodland impossible to cover.

It was Don's idea to set up a road block, stop cars and just see what would happen. Last night Don, Steve and a Mountie did just that from twelve midnight until three in the morning. They stopped eight cars, asked questions and searched them. One car had what they were looking for. When asked if they had a gun, oh my no! Steve opened the door and there was the butt of a gun sticking out of the door. Any shells? Oh my, no! Searching produced a slug and bird shot. What the men claimed was a bundle of clothes turned out to be a herring net. It's not legal for them to be carrying a gun. They were out to kill moose, ducks and geese, and net and jig salmon, all of which are illegal. The guns and net were confiscated and a hearing will be held soon. There will be another road block next week. Maybe they won't find any moose meat, but I'll bet it'll scare a lot of guys.

May, 1956

Have I mentioned before that the Department is trying to get several wild animals to put on display at the annual Grand Falls and Corner Brook fairs? They would like to get a bear cub, lynx, fox and baby moose. It's doubtful that we will obtain all of these, but if any are caught they will be kept in pens and yards *in back of our house* until the fairs in September. I do hope they get a bear cub! A mother and two cubs were reported very near Cormack, but the folks who saw them weren't aware that we would like to capture a couple. Of course, *they* couldn't have caught them anyway. Just imagine, a zoo right out my back window! I'd love it and I'll let you know if and when.

June, 1956

Our yard is completely fenced in and has a fine, sturdy gate out front. This will keep the animals out. But now that the cows won't be coming in, how will the grass be kept clipped? We're certainly not going to buy a lawn mower. Perhaps once a week I'll herd the animals in and then go around after them with a shovel. Very important also is a new well cover. This has been a worry to us as the old one was rotting and I did worry about the children playing around it—to say nothing of that pony that kept climbing on it.

July, 1956

We'll call this "The Zoo That Grew." First there was Wiley Cat, our lynx. When we first met, she was wild and she still is.

One evening we had a couple of strangers in our bathtub. They made quite a mess but were quite at home swimming around. Alf and Reggie are land otters. Lovely creatures with velvety dark fur. Very playful, they spend a great deal of time playing tag and follow-the-leader. But when their favourite dish of trout is served their friendship ceases and a battle for the food commences. We hope to tame them and adapt them to the house as they make fine pets, but so far we just haven't found or taken the time. They have a pen with a nice play area and a tub of water outdoors and are quite happy. My, but they have grown! I suppose we might call them Yankees since they arrived at our home on July 4.

If you folks have been reading Pogo in the Sunday paper I don't have to tell you who "Cinderola" is. He's a black bear, born this spring and about three and a half feet long, nose to tail. We have no intention of taming this guy. He's just being friendly, I know, when he jumps at the cage and growls. He's not to be feared, however, and Don goes right in his pen with him to clean it out. He spends most of his time climbing up the cage, over on a platform and down a ladder. Sometimes he tries to go down his ladder frontwards and this always ends in a tumble on his nose. He's a lot of fun to watch, but he has no respect for cleanliness for either his cage or his food. The otters always do their 'business' in one corner while the bear does it all over, and I do mean all over! He will eat almost anything and Don brought him a treat yesterday. It was ice cream and how he did like it.

But Cinderola isn't the only one who likes ice cream. So does "Johnny." Johnny is a real pet and really is lonely when left alone. He cries when we leave him alone in the house. Johnny is a loveable baby fox. He wasn't so loveable the other day when we returned home to find he had pulled the kitchen curtains down, knocked over a vase and messed three times, once in the sink! He's not exactly house broken, but he has learned a couple of things. For one, he always answers to Johnny and to a whistle. Also, he will retrieve a ball pretty good. He plays for hours with a ball that Don bought him. If I let him, he'd also spend hours tearing papers, magazines, boxes of Kleenex and anything else in the wastebasket. When Johnny has more food than he can eat, he buries it. Buries it in the bed, bookcase, shoes, wastebasket. To get a little rest, I just have to put him outdoors in his pen. He's a real sweetheart when he's asleep on the bed. Prettiest little thing you ever saw.

"Frankie" is pretty, too. She's a dainty little female fox and a very frightened one. She spent her few months of life on a chain at a lumber camp and no one was very friendly with her. She just arrived last Friday and Don still handles her with gloves on as she has very sharp teeth. But we'll get acquainted.

Don's summer assistant, Selby Moss, takes care of the animals and they do require a lot of care. Get the food, prepare it, some raw, some cooked. Fish for the otter, warm milk for the bear and foxes. Fresh water every day for drinking and swimming. Pens must be cleaned at least once a week. The bear and foxes have had loose bowels and we have changed their diet and given them a binding strawberry compound. I guess it is caused by the change in food and surroundings.

"Scruffy" fox arrived July 29. A little bitty fella. We hope to tame him and he has been in the house a couple of times. Johnny would just love to play with these other two foxes but he is so big. He just jumps all over them and bites at them and they are so little they don't quite know how to play with overgrown Johnny. They sure are cute. Johnny does very well retrieving a ball now and he loves it. The only thing, he chews the dickens out of the ball. He's going through his third one now.

September, 1956

A resumé of Don's caribou hunting trip is in order. To end the suspense, he didn't get a caribou. They left Sunday and returned the following Wednesday. It was an extremely difficult trip and there were times when they felt they just couldn't make it through the bush. They almost got a goose, however. They saw several bears and would have shot one if it had been near the end of their trip instead of the beginning. Tuesday they went in ten miles from their camp and spotted a female caribou. John Nichols shot it so we all had a share of the meat. Don was not interested in shooting just any caribou but only one with a proud set of antlers, and so he passed up a twenty-four pointer. Too small!!

It's no good to take a vacation and stay home, as it would be just like any other day. This just can't be avoided. Letters keep coming, people keep knocking, rabbits have to be tended, etc. Also, all of the summer assistants have returned to school. On Friday three men who work on fire patrol in the summer are arriving to work on law enforcement. We believe Uncle Bren, who was here last winter, is returning; we hope so. He's an interesting and likeable man.

Back to caribou. It's delicious. It compares vary favourably with venison and far surpasses moose; tender, fine grained and not strong tasting. We had an eight pound roast and invited the Taylors over for a feast. It was also their first taste of caribou.

October, 1956

Don participated in a major Newfoundland historic event last Friday. Twenty-five ruffed grouse were released here for the first time. The birds were imported from Wisconsin and were released in the Cormack area. I should have said twenty-four were released as one was dead upon arrival. About half of the birds flew off in good shape, some walked away and started eating immediately and there were a few that may not survive.

He has also set up a predator control program and Uncle Bren is setting snares for lynx and fox. Unfortunately, the next day a grouse got in one of the snares. So, one less bird. Don requested the residents in the area not to snare in an effort to protect the birds. The birds were banded and it will certainly be interesting in a couple of years—in even one year—to observe how many have survived. Success could mean good hunting in a few years.

The day after the grouse release Uncle Bren found a dead rabbit lying in a field in this area. After Don examined it, as he does all dead rabbits, he found it *may* have had tularaemia! Not the first time this disease has been found in Newfoundland, but the first time noted on the west coast. The rabbit is being sent to a pathologist in St. John's for further examination. If it is tularaemia, it will mean rabbit catchers will have to take extreme caution in dressing out their rabbits.

That's all for now from Cormack.

Love,
Pearl

Guashawit

On an August night in 1953, Bob Folker and I were awakened from the sound sleep that follows a hard day's work in the bush, with its flies and sweat, by the sound of cans and bottles bouncing from the side and roof of our Sandy Drive camp. A bear was in the dump! The day before, the drive crew had finished sacking this stretch of river and moved on down toward the Exploits. Behind them came the rats and, attracted by the odours of molasses, sugar and other goodies, the local bears as well.

Dumps and sinks are Pandora's boxes for black bears. Because they also visit the camps themselves, they are unwelcome guests to the woods worker. Bears damage camps and break into them sometimes, even when they are occupied. In fact, when Steve Hall was there, a bear did smash the Sandy Drive camp door one night, eventually leaving by a window. I remember well the day Clarence Elms returned from supplying Gordie Butt and Ron Hounsell at Sheffield Lake to tell me excitedly that a she bear had kept Gord and Ron cornered in the Bowater tide-gauging shack the whole of the previous night! The boys had unwittingly encouraged this incident by throwing scraps to a young bear that visited several evenings in a row while they were boiling up on the path between their stores tent and the tent they slept in. But the night before Clarence went over with supplies, the young bear returned with its mother and the old bear walked the boys slowly away from the Coleman stove and their boiled dinner, down the path, up the ramp and into the tiny 4 x 4' shack with its instruments and marking tape measuring water rising and falling beneath. Fortunately, the shack had a door and the boys closed it, but the old bear plunked herself at the foot of the ramp and stayed until daylight while her friendly youngster ripped the stores tent and sampled everything, scattering flour, tins, vegetables and utensils for several yards.

Bears, bears, bears! Most woods workers not only had no love for them but also feared them. They persecuted them, shot at them whenever they could and trapped them. Bears and man got along best when apart.

I had many experiences with bears in Newfoundland, but I never had to kill one. Although I sat up several nights waiting to destroy nuisance bears, for some reason they chose not to return to the damage sites while I was on vigil with a .30 in my hands. On trips in the country when berries were ripening, I saw as many as nine bears in a day's walking and I often watched bears and moose interacting from the lookout behind the Sandy camp. Bears do kill moose and caribou, and during our moose live-trapping operations a bear broke into a trap and killed a calf inside. But regardless of my own interests in bears, I was often assured that they were quite different from the interests and views held by others! These included the teachers at Cormack who watched a bear wander across the schoolyard, a neighbour lady who came crashing into our Cormack home after meeting a bear on the by-road in front of the house, the fish wardens who failed to walk the river between salmon pools as they were supposed to do for fear of meeting bears, woods contractors who lost food from the camp sink and, it sometimes seemed, almost everyone else.

Guashawit tells a story of a bear and something of what attitudes used to be. Today there are changing attitudes expressed by some interest groups in Newfounland society and recent studies on bears there, along with the education and information being shared, are helping to create a more realistic image of the giant black bears of Newfoundland.

"We always went in the towers on the first of June. I mean official. But before June we'd pack in everything we was about to need. All the nails and felt and whatever we needed, my son, to fix up the cabin or tower or anything about. Some years the bears would have all the felt gone, the windows out and the whole works a mess, my son, like you never saw.

"About May the fifteenth Jesse would come over and ask was I ready and I'd say I was itchy to get on with it, and I was too. Around then, 'round the middle of May now, we'd all go in. I always went into the Taubern Lake tower. I was in 'er about twelve years altogether. In the summer, of course.

"It always took two weeks or more to git everything set up and right at the beginnin', that was the time to watch our for the bears, my son. When they comes out of the caves and the clumps they's hungry and they'll eat anything in the world then, my sonnies."

The old man's watery eyes held the faintest glint now. He crossed his legs, fished in his breast pocket behind the pencils for his Target tobacco and papers and slowly rolled a cigarette. Leaning back, he placed a gnarled thumb beneath his right vest-strap and went on yarning. Between his left thumb and forefinger he held a roughly rolled cigarette with a wet end.

"I guess it was somewhere around the last of May, I was goin' up the ladder once a day or so to look around when I saw the bear away over the second rise a-pawin' on the ground at somethin'. I come on down and raffled about in me pack, picked out five shells, took the .30 and went back up to have another look. She was right there, still a-pawin' away, so I looked at me watch and I thought I'd just about have time to git down and git over to where she was and git back before dark, so off I went.

"My sonnies, you sees a long ways with dem glasses. When you set out to look up somethin' that you been watchin' from the glasses, my sonnies, she's out there a wonderful long ways.

"Well now, there was two little rises comin' up between the bigger ones and it took just about a half an hour to get over to where that bitch bear was feedin' and scratchin' about. I s'pose she was feedin' on... on the little emmets—and whatever she rooted up, the nish little grasses about and... and anything at all.

"Now she was a big bitch bear. I squinted about a boulder on the last rise and could just see her back as she moved here and there, maybe, oh, just a good shot away for the .30, about a hundred yards maybe.

"I got down swifflin' along the ground for a ways and then give a squint out at the bear again. Quick as a wink, my son, she jumped and ran off towards a patch of fir, so I up the gun and snaps off four shot so fast as I can oprate her. I hit her all right. She wobbled a bit before she went in the firs. I runned over as quick as I could and just as I got there I hears somethin' at me side. There was a ledge droppin' a few feet to a yella bog below and so I went over and looked down and there was me bear runnin' along the ledge. I give her anudder, me last one. That was all the shells I had.

"In the mornin' I looked about from the tower and went over to the ledge where I fired at her, but she warn't nowhere around. She was hit, all right, but she kept on a-goin' so far as she could!"

The rock crevice reached into the earth for several feet and then widened where the rocks became crumbly. Soil-forming mosses had plugged the light vents leading to ground level above, but air still filtered through. It was dry in the crevice. Hard rains ran off the sloping rock roof. It was seldom that a drop of water filtered through to the den-home.

Guashawit and his sister lay sleeping, curled around with noses hidden and covered between woolly hind legs. In February the little bears were tiny bundles a hundred times smaller than their mother. Now it was almost June and the cubs had grown to eight times their birth weight. The mother bear's cough disturbed the offsprings. Quickly they moved against her, toothless gums muzzling for teats. The mother dropped heavily to her side, blood bubbled from her nose and mouth as she laboured to force short breaths. The wound behind her shoulder was tiny. Only a few of the black hairs had been clipped by the bullet which smashed through the rib cage and settled snugly in the great crature's lung.

The beast lay motionless. Breathing became more difficult. The cubs suckled contentedly, eyes closed, and occasionally bumped the teats with mouth and nose, the better to grip the source of the rich, warm milk. Soon they were asleep.

Two hours passed. The mother bear breathed no longer. A small pool of drying blood lay on the floor of the den beneath her nose.

By morning the cubs were hungrier than they had ever been before. They returned to nurse time and again, but could no longer draw milk from the cold teats. They climbed over the mother, pulling her ears, pawing her nose and head. The adult bear had always retaliated at such actions. She certainly would not tolerate them now. But she did.

The two cubs squealed and whimpered when their attempts to wake the mother failed. They wrestled and fell asleep, each grasping the other, but soon their hunger wakened them.

They became restless and nightfall found them exploring the cave entrance all the way to the out-of-doors, where they had always been forbidden to go.

"It warn't long after that I seen two cubs a-tumblin' over the marsh. They... they was small, nish lookin' little fellers almost too young to be about alone. When I saw dem now I wondered, could it be the cubs from the old she-bear I hit a few days before?

"An dat's just what they was now, my sonnies. Tiny, wee little bears ain't never frolickin' about like that without the old bitch is with 'em. No, my son, that's just what happened. The poor little fellers got so hungry they was forced out to look for food.

"But now they was doin' all right. I watched 'em close and pretty soon a big hawk comes a-floatin' down off the barrens and give a swoop at one of the little fellers. My sonnies, how he did go! An' the, the other one stood up on the hind legs to face him, mind you!"

The old man pounded a fist into the cup of a hand and bent forward to emphasize his point. "They did all right, my son."

Another cigarette rolled and lit, a cup of tea from the steeping pot and the old man with the leathery face and watery eyes leaned back. He drew a thick, crooked-fingered hand over his cheek and tugged at his chin and licked his lips and toothless gums.

"Well now, it was only a day or so after I seen 'em again. They was eatin' away at the nish young shoots of grass and every so often they'd have a go at each other. Now wasn't they de cramp hands. Eatin' away and then they'd be at each other, quick as a flash.

"Then along about an hour or so after I first seen 'em, along comes a old she-bear with one cub. The cub was bigger than the two little fellers but it was still only a cub. Probably the other cub had died maybe or maybe she only had the one. Sometimes a she will only have one cub, you know, and sometimes a she will have three. At first the little fellers ran, but when the old one didn't pay no attention to them they began to come along closer to her. She never give a sign to 'em. Not a sign, my son! Yet they went on almost to her and when she walked on out of sight with her cub the little fellers followed."

To the cubs, the world was very big indeed. There was the wind and all the objects never seen before. At first, when the breeze bent a bush or parted the woolly fur on a cub's coat, the little bears would cuddle the ground tightly and tremble. They ate anything they saw or smelled and so, from eating old-year grasses with the new and many old-year berries, they became ill. No small creature is safe from harmful bacteria and the little bears lost weight. They ate more and grew worse.

On their third day alone, a mother bear happened near with her single cub. Guashawit and his sister saw them and, trembling, they clamoured on shaky legs towards the bitch. Close by they stopped. This was not their mother. They backed away. The bitch paid no attention to the orphans though she was aware of them.

The bigger cub bounded towards the twins and they played but the orphans were no match. Sickly and weak, they bawled when tripped over or mauled by the larger animal. The bitch bear grunted. She called to the three cubs. They moved up to her and she nursed them all.

The adopted cubs grew swiftly. In four weeks' time they were nearly as big as the bitch's own cub.

As they grew up together, the cubs learned from the bitch how to find the kinds of food they liked. They overturned rotted logs to find beetles and beetle larvae. They ate ants with sawdust and wood chips, and grasses, sedges, leaves, berries, carrion and mice. The adult showed them where to find honey and how to fish for the spawning salmon and trout.

Playful cubs learn quickly, but they would learn still more quickly if they were more attentive. Playing tag and wrestling in trees, on the ground and in the water, the cubs would be alternately bruised and wet. One day, Guashawit had his ear torn by the bitch's playful cub. Blood oozed out and matted the woolly hair on Guashawit's neck and under his chin. The adult bear noticed the wound and with her powerful claws tore the bark of a fir tree, licked the pungent sap and transferred it to the little bear's ear.

Often the mother had to discipline her cubs, teaching them that foolishness can mean injury or death. Thus all three cubs often received heavy blows and cuffs from the mother bear, and though they would whimper or bawl loudly at such times they learned to respect the bitch and her lessons. When the bitch was ready to breed in the cubs' second year, the younger animals were prepared to live by themselves.

The cubs learned to feed on what was available at each season, so in the fall the bitch moved her tribe to the berry barrens where for several weeks they put on quantities of fat. As winter approached, the old bear sought a resting place and found one beneath three trees that had fallen across each other in a blow-down area. There the bears made themselves comfortable, fashioning nest beds from grasses and sedges in the hollows of the ground. Winter came and the bears slept.

By June of their second year the cubs were alone. The bitch had abandoned them, slapping them back and forcing them to stay behind. She would not return.

Guashawit travelled with his twin and the other cub until fall. Then he left them, the last of his playing days over. He spent the winter, except for a warm period of two weeks in January, under a windfall covered with snow.

In the spring Guashawit travelled widely, seeking food of any kind. His travels brought him to a woods camp. The camp had not yet been opened this spring and careful woodsmen, thinking of bears, had boarded windows and doors of all the buildings. Sniffing around the buildings, Guashawit soon picked out the storeroom and promptly began to tear the boards loose from the windows with his powerful forepaws.

One smash shattered the glass and Guashawit squeezed through, grunting. He was almost too big. Here was a barrel of salt meat, barrels of flour, tins of fruit and vegetables and dried fruit. Guashawit bit into the cans and lapped at the draining juices, threw flour about with great sweeps of his forepaws and ate the salty meat and dried fruits. The dishes, stacked neatly on cupboard shelves, puzzled him and he picked them up and stacked them along the wall, breaking some in the process. Then, satisfied and filled, he broke down a door and left. Bears prefer to have separate entrances and exits and, besides, Guashawit might well have been too big for the window now.

Guashawit destroyed parts of many camps in his lifetime. He was shot at and wounded but balsam and spruce gum and water helped to heal his wound.

Early each summer Guashawit sought out females ready to mate. Sometimes he fought other males. Great brawling battles he fought and won, for he was larger than any of the bears he fought.

Then one late summer day Guashawit happened to roam near the place of his birth.

❧

"You talk about bears! I'll tell you a bear story! It was the last year I was in at Taubern Lake and it was in the heat of the summer,

August month it was. I'd only seen four or five bears all summer. One was around the camp and so I killed 'un. Late at night I got up and lookin' out the door I could just make 'un out, but I got 'un with one shot."

The old man ran the back of his hand across his mouth and recrossed his legs. "But dat's another bear story. I saw this big bear from the tower early in the mornin'. He was a dog, I could see from his hump and a big dog too. Down I got, grabbed me .30 and a pack and off after him I goes. The bear was feedin' on berries now and this dog, my son, was busy takin' berries, bushes and everything. I creeped up the last ways a-squintin' about each boulder to mark him down ahead and kinda watch his movements a bit. The wind, my sonnies, was just right, blowin' in to me, not real strong, but jus shiftin' along quiet.

"An' when I peeked around the last rock, he was right there, boy, not fifty foot away an' eatin' the hurts berries so fast as he could gulp 'em down. He burped, my son, and you coulda heard it all the way to Port Blandford if the wind was right.

"I ups me gun and aims right for the ear and squeezes and he jus' lops over, my son, as nice as you like it. A couple of twitches of the hind legs and he was quiet as a mouse. One shot, my sonnies!

"It was about the middle of the mornin' then and I took out me knife and panched 'im and skinned back off the hind quarters and scalped off the meat. My son, wasn't he fat now! Jus like de pig. I stuffed the nish parts down in me pack and piled meat on top and packed it right out past the tower and out to the railroad. That's seven miles out from the tower, my son. I flagged down a speeder after a bit and went on in to Clarenville. Then in the mornin', I went back in with Al, me son, and one of his buddies and they carried out some more. They was sixty pounds of meat in me pack and Al and his buddy took out twice as much. The rest we had to leave because de heat was turnin' it."

If It's Good For A Scoff

There was a saying about the outports of Newfoundland that "If it's good for a scoff, kill it and eat it. If it's not good for a scoff, kill it for it ain't worth livin'." It's not strange that such a saying arose from the utilitarian outlook of a hardy people who for hundreds of years had to depend upon nature's resources for their lives and who learned of innumerable ways to harvest those resources at various times of the year. Whether cod or whales, rabbits or caribou; whether mud trout or moose, it was all the same. Turrs were the 'finest kind' and so, to some, were bull birds and gulls. The ways of a people that had been successful over generations should not be expected to change with the shrill cries of radical environmentalists or from the pen of animal rights and animal welfare moralists overnight. Maybe with another generation or two some different attitudes would arise, but patience was required in the 1950s and, I believe, for outsiders it still is today.

Once in a while each of us experiences the personal exhilaration of knowing a truly honest person. My friend Art Taylor was just such a man.

One fall morning I walked into the Co-op store Al managed, to find him downcast, really glum. His usual cheerfulness, his usual bright smile and the twinkle that was usually in his eyes were not present. Today there was no cheer, no smile and no twinkle.

"You got to arrest me," he said, looking straight at me.

"Don't be silly," I replied. "What did you ever do to make you say such a thing?"

"I killed two moose yesterday," he said. "Johnnie and me were walkin' down over the burn toward Harriman's Brook, you know, and up jumped a big old cow moose. I ups and aims and fires. But the moose was still after standing, so I fired again just as Johnnie started hollering." He paused for a moment, shaking his head. "I must of blinked when I fired first because I'd shot two. The cow must of dropped and the calf must of been behind her and when I saw the calf I thought I'd missed! So arrest me," he said, "you gotta do what's your job to do."

Well, I could just see them. Art with a lunchpack on his back, carrying his old '92 Winchester with the propped up rear sight and Johnnie with his little pack and an ax over his shoulder. Neither was a hunter, but moose were plentiful and you didn't have to be much of hunter to find one. Art had bought a license and, like many others, the two would hunt together, kill one moose and split it between them. Split it down, panch it and quarter it, all with an ax. There would be plenty of meat for two small families when you also had a bit of tinned and salt meat, salt cod and, in their particular cases, an occasional hen from flocks of egg layers they both kept penned from foxes and lynx in their back yards.

There they were, down over the east slope of the burn headed toward the brook, and there was the moose! Art would blink when the rifle discharged too and in his excitement would quickly try and dispatch the animal he had 'missed' with a second shot as Johnnie, whose eyes were open *all* the time, shouted in desperation for Art not to shoot. But Art wouldn't hear what Johnnie shouted when his heart was making enough noise to drown out most every other sound around except the rifle shot, so 'blam' went the rifle and down went the calf.

"Art," I said, "tell Johnnie to come in the office and buy a license. It was an accident and even if I wanted to charge you, I couldn't get any magistrate around to find you guilty after you told him your story. Anyway, I don't want to charge you. Still, we should cover the two moose with licenses, so Johnnie should buy one." And Johnnie did.

Art would never, ever squeal, not on anyone. Yet if he knew of a moose being killed illegally and if he knew it to be unnecessary for that person, as far as an actual need, it was a measure of his integrity that he would let me know somehow. Sometimes he obtained information from others passing through the community, but most often he simply observed that "Missus Toles was in and stocked up on jars and a bit of pork." Or maybe, "Missus Shephard and Arno are down with summer complaint." In this latter instance, I was to assume that the family was consuming too much fresh meat. Or at least, consuming without adding enough pepper! The former, of course, would be obvious. Missus Toles would be busy bottling fresh meat.

It was in just such a manner that I learned one day that Arno had indeed killed still another of his many illegally taken moose. He worked part-time in summer on the highroad, but for the rest of the year, except for an occasional odd job about the area or a week or so in a woods camp or when he was replenishing his wood supply, he was at loose ends and this meant, too often, killing moose which, except for the little he and his wife ate, he sold or gave away. There were just the two of them, Arno and his wife Annie. Now she was thought to be a little strange by some in the community and Arno himself suffered from a nervous temperament excused by the common knowledge that he had suffered severe head wounds at Normandy. It was in part because of these personal peculiarities and characteristics that Arno presented a somewhat more difficult problem than some others that were near regular violators. Once, a year before I came to Cormack, Arno was fined. Seventy-five dollars it was then; transferred from his pocket (Welfare) to another office of the Crown (to Natural Resources). This seemed to me to be much like a bookkeeping problem or an internal transfer of funds from one Ministry to another that penalized the welfare recipient and the average taxpayer since, in my view, welfare funds shouldn't be used to pay for fines. Nor, thought I, should court costs be tallied up for such an infraction. But how to impress? How to teach? These were questions one had to try and answer.

After I arrived on the scene, the first moose Arno killed in addition to legal ones was handled differently. It was seized and distributed (which Arno would have done anyway) and the magistrate cooperated with a stern lecture and a dire warning of future consequences if Arno repeated such acts, then ended with a suspended sentence.

Now, however, the suspension was no longer in effect and Arno and Annie suffered from the summer complaint so I drove to Deer Lake to get Corporal Hogan to join me for a trip to Arno's house. On arriving we found Annie by herself and since she normally responded to questions with a giggle, Hogan dispensed with the routine and settled on a simple, "Annie, we're gonna search for Arno's moose." And so we did. In the shed, in the root cellar and, carefully (as Annie served us tea), in the house. But there was no moose and no moose meat, although I thought I could smell cooked moose right there in the kitchen. Before we had finished our tea,

Arno drove in the yard in his battered old International rig and the Corporal and I went out to greet him.

"Arno," the Corporal said, "we've come to take your moose."

Arno didn't appear surprised at this since he was, by this time, not unused to such visits and such information emanating from those charged with enforcing the game laws. He walked past us straight for his shed.

"She's over here," he said, throwing open the double doors. As they opened, he shouted, "Lord Jesus, somebody stole me moose!"

With that he started looking ever so carefully around the shed; lifting a shovel here and an ax there, as if perhaps a whole moose might just be hidden underneath one of them somewhere.

"She was here when I left, Corporal," he said wonderingly. "I left her here except for a quarter. She was hanging from right up there," and he pointed to the juniper pole strung across up under the shed roof. "Now," he said, looking at the two of us sort of innocently, "she's gone."

This was indeed a wonder. Arno had had a moose for sure, but where was it now? I suggested maybe we should return to the kitchen and finish our interrupted tea and try and talk it out. Surely Arno or Annie would have some idea of where it could have gone; some little idea, maybe. Four hundred pounds of moose meat doesn't leave without help. At least, not quickly it doesn't. We ventured back into the kitchen with the wise old Corporal asking questions in his rapid fire speech and Arno, a foot shorter than the Corporal but chippy as a jay bird, answering back honestly and talking of the wonder of the vanished moose all at the same time.

Back in the house the Corporal leaned against a covered puncheon that reeked of brew working off while I sat down at the table and Annie refilled our mugs as well as one for Arno.

"Wouldn't have any brew around, would you, Arno?" the Corporal asked, patting the puncheon with both hands.

"No sir," said Arno, seriously, his black eyes peering from under bushy eyebrows straight at the Corporal.

The Corporal pushed away from the smelly puncheon and, joining us at the table, heaved a sigh and looked at me, shaking his head. He didn't have any ideas about the moose any more than I did or, apparently, than Arno did, and he had only wanted to let Arno know that the puncheon of brew wasn't a secret.

Just then Arno's neighbour from across the by-road, one Hilbert Cassidy, a bachelor, appeared at the kitchen door and beckoned to Arno with a crooked finger to come outside so Arno stood up quickly and dodged out the door to see Hilbert. In less than a minute he was back.

"Corporal," he shouted excitedly, "I found me moose!"

Up we got and followed Arno out directly to the wood pile where Hilbert was busy chucking chunks off three quarters of moose meat. Lucky Arno to have such a friend to go to the effort of hiding an illegal moose for him! Luckier still to have recovered it so the game warden would seize it and distribute it about the community, saving Arno the trouble!

One of Art's favourite expressions used to help us locate illegal kills he might know about, and which were left lying about for a time for one reason or another, was to "follow the crows and hold your nose." This we often did, sometime finding a carcass in a place too close to the road (within smelling distance, for instance) so that we had to dispose of it by some means. Maybe we'd bury it or using a set of tackle blocks, haul it away, or sometimes we'd split it and dump quick lime in the gut cavity. One late September evening after tea it wasn't one of these usual bits of information we got but a really different type; much more direct than usual.

"Been a big, black Cadillac with New Jersey plates going over the road lately," Art said, "and old Jimmy John is in the back seat."

"Is that right?" I said. "Have you seen it lately?"

"Just stopped here for gas," Art said. "My son, do you know how much gas them Cadillacs use?"

"Comin' or goin'?" I asked, referring to the Cadillac.

"They uses the same both ways," he said. "No, seriously b'y, they just went out toward Big Falls."

This was, it seemed to me, to be well worth checking into. It was only late September and our split and zoned moose season was open in the interior but nowhere was it open on the west coast. I drove up to the bunkhouse and got Uncle Bren Tilley, who was as usual in the process of rolling a sloppy Target cigarette, to accompany me out over the highroad.

It was always best to be accompanied by someone, even one who rolled wrinkled Targets and yarned a lot. Witnesses were important but, more to the point, two men, even two such as Bren and me, that is, one old yarner and one younger listener, made for a greater degree of safety. Alone, I had been driven off the road by pulp trucks, shot at, threatened and near run over as I was changing a tire, but when there were two of us, we made out much better and sometimes the enforcement procedures would be almost amiable. Of course, even when I was alone I had friendly chats and good experiences with some game violators on occasion, but if one or more poachers wanted trouble they'd be more likely to look for it when an officer was alone.

Uniforms also helped. There is something about a uniform that commands attention if not always respect. I did have my uniform on the evening that I picked up Uncle Bren and took off in the old Fargo looking for a black Cadillac with Jersey plates. Since it was probably the only one in Newfoundland it shouldn't be hard to find and since she wouldn't have but inches of clearance she should be on or near the highroad. So it was.

Bren and I were just bumping over Harriman's Brook bridge and Bren had just allowed as how the Fargo rode and bumped "just like (goin' through) Baccalieu Tickle" when up ahead of us, right in the middle of the road, was a man, rifle to his shoulder, aiming at a big cow moose that stood about fifty yards down from him, also in the middle of the road, looking right at the man. I slammed on the brakes, blew the horn and hollered out the window at the man, "Don't shoot that moose!"

Well, he lowered his rifle and turned back to look at us as we drove up to him. "I wasn't gonna shoot," he said, sort of defensively, "we already got one with no horns. Now we're looking for one *with* horns!"

Well talk about surprised! Here was a man dressed in new red mackinaw trousers and jacket with a cartridge belt wrapped around him and what I recognized as a Remington game master that looked as though it just came off the shelf, standing *in* the road admitting he had already shot a moose in an area where the moose season wouldn't be open for more than a month!

We pulled ahead a few yards to an old highway push-off now grown up with birches and fir, turned in and found ourselves hood to hood with the Cadillac. Next to it stood two near-carbon copies of the man in the road, each decked out in spanking new hunting clothes and fancy boots, each weighted down with a few pounds of shells in cartridge belts and each carrying expensive and shiny semi-automatic rifles. Like the man in the road who strolled in by the truck as Uncle Bren and I got out, each was also heavy bearded, dark and heavy-set. "Hit men on a holiday," I thought. Maybe there's a body in the trunk!

Jimmy John was in the back seat of the Caddy. While Uncle Bren went over to question him I checked the hunters' non-resident licenses, accompanying maps and regulatory information. All were purchased in Port-aux-Basques at the RCMP detachment. All of the men had Italian sounding names and they all had the appropriate information clearly indicating that they were, at that time, about 150 miles by road from any open moose zone.

"You said you had one moose without horns," I said to the man who had been on the road. "Where is it now?"

"In the trunk," he said, just as if it was common for everyone to stuff moose (or other dead bodies?) in the trunks of cars.

"I don't believe it," I said. "Open it up."

He opened it and there was indeed a body in the trunk! Just where the Mafia might put one. It was a smallish calf and it stunk. It even had the head left on it, all curled up and squeezed in. It had been panched, but not panched cleanly and it had been stuffed in the trunk with no air! I looked around at them, all three standing sober-faced and motionless, watching me. Human predators on other humans, perhaps; lost in the real wild world. Caricatures of the worst of humankind when outside Jersey City, I thought.

"Jimmy John said this was sweet ground here," one of them said. I looked at Jimmy standing outside the car with Bren now. He was grinning. He knew the law and he knew he was pretty safe from any consequences. He'd probably made a pocket full of money and accumulated a few forty ouncers from these yahoos. Jimmy had good reason to grin.

The next night Bren and I were mentioned on the Gerald S. Doyle News Bulletin. That Americans from New Jersey had been caught hunting boldly in an illegal area and with a rotting calf moose stuffed in the trunk besides made for great talk, dozens of crude jokes and much laughter for days in and around Cormack.

We had seized rifles, ammunition *and* the Cadillac and locked it all up in the RCMP detachment garage and office at Deer Lake for a couple of days until Magistrate White could hear the case in Corner Brook, inconveniencing the trio more than a little.

The Mafia-moose boys were eventually fined appropriately and lost their rotten little moose. They were also appraised of the regulations and lectured on what they could and could not do as only Jack White could lecture! We then contacted our Natural Resources staff in Grand Falls and steered the 'hit men' to Badger where they entered the country to a legal hunting area but also where they were even more poorly suited for travelling. It was an environment with roads the like of which almost prevented their Cadillac from moving. So they left the Island.

Jimmy John had stood smiling at the hearing while he was hammered with threats from the magistrate, but he was the only real winner. Our regulations couldn't reach him at the time and Jimmy had great fun. He even thought Magistrate White was a 'real nice feller.'

There were magistrates and there were magistrates. In 1957 I wrote in a confidential report to the Director of Wildlife that, "Some of the newly appointed men appear to have no sympathy for the game violators and some of the older magistrates appear to have little sympathy for the game or for the Wildlife Officer."

One day in early fall over a week before the rabbit snaring season was to open, I began following a newly blazed trail leading from a half-ton rig parked on Riverside Road, through a fifteen—twenty-year-old cutover thickly regenerating with fir. There were two or three snares tailed along every rabbit lead, dozens and dozens of them as I walked, eventually, well over a mile. I heard voices, so I slowed down and shortly I stood within a few yards of two men tailing slips on either side of their blazed path. A young fellow of about twelve or so stood holding an ax in one hand and rabbit wire in the other.

"You boys about to catch a few rabbits, I guess," I said.

They turned quickly and the two men stood up. "It's the damned game warden," said one.

After talking a bit I learned that they both worked at Bowaters Mill in Corner Brook and were going to tail their slips a week before the season since that would allow them to revisit on their next off-day (shift work at the mill meant there was always one day a week for poaching) which would be opening day. This would allow them to have a few braces of rabbits for sale before any other rabbit catcher who might be following the rules could have them.

Anyway, I walked back along their line with them that evening and helped them take up every one of the 119 slips and told them I was laying charges. I kept their slips for the hearing and seized their single barrel H&R 12 gauge.

Now, it all sounds cut and dried. Commercial rabbit catchers were beating the legal opening by a week and also carrying a firearm contrary to a section of our regulations. But when we appeared a week later before a magistrate in Corner Brook, the magistrate commiserated from the Bench with these gentlemen and lectured *me* for bringing these men before him! Of course he had to find them guilty, but he didn't fine them, he just handed them short suspended sentences and warned them that they should be sharp enough to avoid me.

On another occasion I had laid charges against two commercial poachers in early December. Both drove new vehicles and held good paying jobs, but the magistrate lectured me about bringing such cases before him just before Christmas and postponed our adventure until January 8.

Often magistrates would counsel defendants on how to answer questions from those prosecuting and sometimes even advised them not to answer. On innumerable occasions they returned seized firearms that, under the Act, should have been confiscated.

Still, Magistrate White held out no olive branches for game law violators. I once brought a man before him charged with using No. 4, 12 gauge shot for moose and carrying a loaded firearm on the main road. Now this man had a big family and I had already asked the magistrate not to fine the fellow since my findings had shown that he was truly ignorant of what he was doing and would be unlikely to repeat the behaviour. He also had eleven children and was drawing welfare; yet he had purchased a license, an unusual event. It was to be a suspended sentence (with a lecture), but the defendant almost blew it. When the magistrate, for clarification, asked what in the world he was doing with No. 4 shot in his shotgun after moose, the accused replied, dishonestly, since he had already admitted he was hunting moose, that he was shooting woodpeckers.

Mr. White was a birder. He liked birds and he despised the killing of birds. The magistrate rose up from behind the bench and I thought he'd keep on rising right up through the roof. He was livid.

"Shooting woodpeckers!" he shouted. He proceeded to cut the poor man to ribbons using all manner of language almost improper for such adjudicators and causing the United Church parson, who was sitting in the back of the room looking after the defendant who was a member of his flock, to admonish him with a "Tut, tut, tut!"

For several years I dealt with Magistrate White, who was good man and, if I recall correctly, a former newspaperman. I also dealt with several other judges and at least two I knew were consistent in their unswerving, unequivocal and dedicated devotion to erratic judgements in relation to wildlife matters. All wildlife and RCMP officers did their best to avoid those fellows whose Utopian social views made a mockery of both our regulations and our wildlife. I don't know what the backgrounds were of the several magistrates we worked with, but some had been school teachers and many were, in addition to their previous professions or careers, powerful good Liberals! Then, too, their knowledge of law and jurisprudence was clearly not extraordinary, which meant that peace officers had to have considerable faith in the integrity and honesty of these laymen judges. Men who, through politics in most cases, had been made overseers of the populace for all matter of civil and criminal acts perpetrated by their fellow citizens. It took a large bundle of faith on the part of Mounties and Wildlife Officers too. Faith that was seldom rewarded with punishment fitting the crimes.

There was another man besides Art Taylor who provided helpful information for us in a somewhat indirect manner. He would stop his truck in front of the office and come in for a brief three or four minutes time of day chat. On leaving, he would casually mention the crows flocking about "a hundred yards this side of the turn at the base of Birchy Ridge on the left-hand side of the road." A good man was Howard and I appreciated his oblique references.

Dave Pike and I followed one up one evening and after awhile we located four quarters of moose in the alders just off the highroad. It was supposed to rain that night and though first we thought we might drive the truck off the road half a mile back toward Big Falls and wait in the alders by the meat, we later decided to split up, thinking it might be an all night vigil. We thought we'd stake out in shifts and avoid the chance of the culprits seeing the truck or its tracks on what was soon to be a muddy road. It was seven in the evening when Dave took the first watch. I was to return by midnight and relieve him until early morning. Dave stayed and I left and it began to rain. It rained buckets, in fact, and after I had a cup of tea and a biscuit in our snug Cormack living room my conscience wouldn't let me read, relax or work on a monthly report that was due, so shortly after nine o'clock I left the house well suited up for a soggy October night and headed out over the highroad to relieve Dave a couple of hours early, thinking he surely must be soaked.

And soaked he was, but not just from the rain. It turned out that at about 9 p.m., as Dave huddled in the bushes sitting on a pair of rubberized gloves to keep his bottom dry, a van stopped opposite him and a man got out and strolled across the road. He stopped directly over the four quarters of meat, and also over a hunched-up Dave. After a minute or two that seemed like hours to Dave, the man unzipped his pants and relieved his distended bladder, careful to aim close to, but not on, the meat. Unfortunately for Dave, by narrowly missing the quartered moose, the stream landed directly on him! But good old intrepid Dave kept his head lowered and took it, never moving and barely breathing lest he give himself away. After a shake or two and zipping up his trousers, the man turned and strolled casually back to the van, got in and soon the van moved away on up the Ridge. Of course Dave thought he'd been seen and that the jig was up, but not so. Only four or five minutes later the van came back down the Ridge, slowly pulling alongside the illegal moose meat and stopped. The driver, who had shortly before relieved himself on poor Dave, got out and opened the rear doors of the van and he and his partner, a gentleman with a hook attached to the stub of his lower left arm, came over and down into the shrubbery. Each of them reached and struggled to lift a quarter to their shoulders and then they lugged them back to the van and dropped the meat inside the truck. It was then that Dave made his presence known!

I guess it was the element of surprise that startled the poachers and made them more submissive than one would have expected, for Dave had no trouble at all and by the time I arrived they were, all three, in the van with the moose meat, and Dave was 'bringing them in.'

Now this was not Dave's only experience with this sort of thing, though he certainly had no natural propensity for being in such a position, I'm sure. He was, however, actually baptised his very first day on the job by a lynx! We had gone directly from the train station out to Little Falls Brook to a cubby set I had not checked that day and when we got there we found the No. 2 jump was missing along with the drag, so I cautioned Dave not to walk around while I carefully searched the low growth shrubbery. You can easily step on a lynx for they seldom fight traps or slips. When even a small amount of pressure is sensed on a front paw, the animal will lie down and wait. I once took an adult animal in a rabbit slip with only an alder stick attached. It laid down about ten feet from where its curiosity had caused it to paw the slip glinting in the moonlight, after the stick had become snagged slightly in the *Kalmia*. On another occasion I took a young animal in a No. O Victor long spring (weasel) trap and it was caught only by a toe. It was sitting and waiting, with its paw held up slightly, the tiny trap on its toe and the ring wired to a little stick. Unless accidentally taken by the hind foot, lynx seldom move more than a few yards when caught, but if taken by a hind foot they will sometimes drag for a considerable distance. In a snare they usually lunge only once, but *all* cats succumb very quickly and quietly in neck snares.

I once did step on the foot of a lynx which had moved a few feet into the withy bushes and had my logans scratched in a wink, however, so on Dave's first day I cautioned him to be careful, stand still and wait. Besides, he was still dressed in a suit and had oxfords on!

After a minute or so of searching carefully about, I heard water running and Dave exclaimed, "What the?" I turned and he was looking up where the lynx was crouched next to the trunk, on a low branch of a spruce tree. Poor Dave was directly under the lynx which was, no doubt, nervous because of us and was relieving itself. The trap chain and drag hung down, resting against the opposite side of the tree so we hadn't noticed them and, besides, you seldom look up to find a lynx.

One of our more humorous incidents with lynx occurred one late fall evening when Dave, Uncle Bren and I were accompanied by Jack Saunders, who was just beginning his Newfoundland lynx study. We had enjoyed a busy afternoon, having tested out "Spike," a new to us but really an old cat hound recently imported from Nova Scotia to track lynx, by letting a tagged lynx run off directly in front of the dog and then releasing him. Spike howled beautifully for maybe four minutes and then stopped. It was dead quiet until we heard him trotting through the brush back of us where he came up, panting and sat down alongside. Spike never did run a lynx to bay, but we kept him in dog food, as a boarder, anyway. He seemed to enjoy people.

We had also tied up, processed and released a second lynx that afternoon. Since there were four of us, the tying, measuring and tagging and other processing of data was really quite simple. One man can easily tie up a lynx without injury to himself if he's careful. I have done it several times. I had even issued step-by-step instructions to staff in the district, although there were a couple of holdouts who didn't want to become that intimate with these lovely animals. Today, however, with four of us, we had handled two lynx by late afternoon with only one set left to check and this was only about a mile from the by-road. But wouldn't you know it! On reaching the trap site we found we had a third cat. We had taken three in six traps and the sets had been checked only forty-eight hours before.

It was nearly dark when we arrived at cat number three and in our haste to do all that had to be done with the critter and release it, we were careless enough to allow its forepaws to slip out of our tie after the trap was removed. Unfortunately, Uncle Bren was closest to the working end of the lynx and wasn't quite quick enough to jump completely away when the animal made a flashing grab with both paws. Catching the top of Uncle Bren's left logan, the animal's claws held tightly while Bren, holding on to a small fir with his hands, tried to pull his leg free. It was only a matter of seconds before I placed an alder stick before the lynx's head and it grabbed on, sinking its canines deeply enough to prevent it from opening its mouth again for a few moments. We were able to slip a bit of light rope around each front leg, tighten the knots and lift the paws from Bren's boot. Still it seemed like a long time to Bren and in the Co-op store that night he told all and sundry of his close call with the lynx and how all the rest of us "stood round salootin'" while he struggled vainly to free himself. Of course, he had the claw mark on his logans for proof. He had them on his legs, too, but no on asked him to haul his britches and longjohns up to see.

Back in the mid-fifties no on had yet succeeded in getting lynx to breed and produce offspring in captivity. It was to be a few years before successes in Alberta were to be followed by Eldon Pace in Nova Scotia and others elsewhere. I was trying, however. I changed diets from commercial cat food to full wild meat and used various combinations with vitamins, but nothing worked. I thought maybe the problem might be a behaviourial one rather than one related to nutrition, so I enlarged the pens and connecting runway for one of the adult males and one of the females we were holding, thinking spacial aspects might be involved. Soon after this I had an idea that maybe the cats should kill their own food, so I tried putting live rabbits in their pens at night, which they did indeed kill and eat. I also tried a chicken. Why, I don't know, because there are precious few chickens in Newfoundland lynx country. It was a Rhode Island Red and I got it from Art Taylor's flock for, I think, two dollars. I chucked the old hen in the female's pen along with some scratch grain and watched from a distance. The old bird walked about, clucking and pecking at the scratch quite as if it was socializing with its own kind and apparently in no fear of the cat. The poor lynx, on the other hand, appeared terrified of the chicken and kept far back inside its covered box area. When I eventually looked in with a flashlight, the trembling cat was casting wary glances at the hen while the clucking old fowl kept on filling her crop with scratch. I left them together for three days without feeding the female lynx anything else, but she wouldn't go near the chicken. I then gave the hen back to Art and two dollars went back to petty cash. It did turn out later that chicken in a lynx's diet would be important in the first captive breeding work, so I had the right train, quite by accident, but I was clearly on the wrong track!

When we first began to handle lynx we thought it would be necessary to immobilize them, so Doug Pimlott obtained the data on a curare derivative drug which, in 1955, was being used with a number of wild animals. My first try with it was on a lynx in one of our traps back of Cormack. Uncle Bren and I were together that day and I measured the liquid out carefully in a syringe as Uncle Bren looked on sceptically. I was able to keep to the rear of the cat that was lying quietly by us and I gingerly jammed the needle in its rump, squeezing the stuff into the muscle, or so I thought. Bren and I set about to boil the kettle. We made a fire, boiled up, ate and still the lynx showed no sign of the drug taking effect. Yet the directions and all the literature were quite clear on the time and the dosage. Maybe my injection was only subcutaneous and maybe I hadn't penetrated muscle tissue at all.

"My sonnies," said Bren, "that lynx isn't goin' to go to sleep wid dat stuff."

"Oh, yes she is," I said. "I'm giving her another shot and this time I'll punch her well in the butt muscle." I did and sure enough, in a few moments Mrs. Lynx began to blink and had trouble holding her head up. Soon we took the trap from her undamaged paw. (In all of our trapping and marking we damaged only two lynx paws, breaking toes in each, and still one of these animals was retrapped twice after the damage occurred.) We did the weighing and measuring and all the other goodies, squeezed a Ketchum tag in one ear and kept track of our watches for her to begin to come around. After an hour it seemed clear she was not going to regain consciousness very quickly and Uncle Bren was certain I'd killed her. But, no, I could detect her heartbeat. Not too rapid and not too strong, but beating nonetheless. I decided to tie her up to a stick to lug her back to the bunkhouse where we'd put her in our holding box, for she might well freeze with lowered respiration and circulation if she didn't come around that afternoon. This we did and in the morning the cat was indeed awake and seemed fit as a fiddle, watching our every move, alert and sharp. We took her back near the by-road and released her later in the day, though I did have some concern that we might be letting an animal loose with brain damage. Uncle Bren assured me, however, that a lynx that could run out of the box like she did was clearly "first rate."

After this we began tying the cats up and handling them without drugs.

But it was moose that took up so much of our time. Doug Pimlott had initiated moose studies in Newfoundland in 1951, and by 1953 I had joined the moose team. Moose were first introduced, apparently unsuccessfully, into Newfoundland in 1878. The high density population of the fifties was the probable result of releasing only two males and two females from New Brunswick in 1904.

In 1953 Bob Folker and I had forty-seven moose observations from a single observation point in one day (three hours of observing) and since we saw twenty-seven different animals during the hour and a half observation period in the morning, at least twenty-seven must have been different animals. On the first morning of the open season in 1957, I checked twenty legal kills along a twenty-one mile stretch of road east from Cormack to Hampden turnoff. From the air our density indices were so high that in one area of central Newfoundland a multiple moose season was conducted to help lower their numbers and reduce the damage caused by moose to fir regeneration. Between 1935, when the first open season was declared, and 1980, about 200,000 animals were know to have been legally killed. The specific economic benefits, combined with the subsistence benefits provided by moose for Newfoundland and its people were, indeed, little short of miraculous.

But moose caused problems too. They ate turnip tops and this meant farmers became upset and sometimes demanded compensation for losses. In one instance it took a full afternoon's discussion and a half case of Jockey before one farmer from

Pasadena agreed that his losses were closer to a bushel than they were to the four tons he had claimed in his letter to the Minister. Still, other damage problems were often more difficult to handle, even with RCMP involvement, especially when automobiles and lives were at stake. Many moose were killed from collisions with trains and logging trucks and others were left dead or wounded by poachers if they were in delicate places. It sometimes seemed that we were always hauling dead moose or burying or chopping open and liming or putting down injured animals. In fact, moose got to be a real bore after the first few experiences. After all, they're heavy and decomposing moose doesn't smell all that great.

One night shortly after midnight, following several hours of yarning at the bunkhouse with Captain Walters, Steve Hall and Uncle Bren, I had just dropped off to sleep when a knock woke me up. I went to the door to find Captain Walters, who said that a couple of men returning from salmon fishing at Big Falls had stopped when they saw the light to report that they had hit and injured a moose at Goose Bog. Pretty late for salmon fishing, of course, but the honourable fishermen allowed as how they had stayed with a couple of friends camped at Big Falls for a drink before returning, and this was believable.

I got dressed and followed the fishermen out to Goose Bog, where they pointed to the spot where the collision had taken place that smashed their right fender and headlight. Harry and I took off across the bog: he with a five cell flashlight and me with my .32 WCF. About a quarter of the way across we stopped and flashed the area ahead of us and around the edges. Sure enough, at the far end of the marsh a cow struggled to pull itself up. It appeared to have a broken back but we didn't know how badly it was hurt or how fast it might be able to travel. Besides, it was at the edge of thick tuckamore and if it got inside we'd surely not be able to dispose of it this night. We'd better take a chance on a hundred yard shot than to push her.

"Shine the light over my shoulder and hit the moose on the neck and head with the beam," I said to Harry, who quickly complied. I then raised the rifle and moved to get enough light across the top of the barrel to see, squeezed a shot away and down went the moose. I'd hit her in the neck.

"I'll bet money you've done this before," chuckled Harry. But I hadn't.

A wildlife biologist was expected to do a lot of things, at least by some people. There had never been such a district person in

Newfoundland before and the some 10,000 square miles from Port aux Basques to St. Anthony and east near to Buchans held a lot of people with a lot of different ideas about what such a biologist should do or even could do.

One evening three little kids, probably seven to ten years of age, came over to the house. The boy, who was the oldest or at least the biggest, held a puppy which looked droopy and sad as mauled puppies sometimes do.

"Could ya git the 'ook out of 'is mouth?" the little boy asked.

I looked carefully at the pup's mouth and there in the lower lip was a small trout hook part way through his lower lip. It had entered from the outside, having been caught when the kids were troutin' at the bridge near us and they had cut off the line attached. Only the knot and a bit of worm showed on the shank.

It was a fairly simple matter for Pearl to hold the puppy tightly while I shoved the hook all the way through, nipped off the barb with pliers and backed the shank out. To the kids it was a near miracle, however. Later, many years later, as I handed an endorsed check to a new teller in a Bank of Montreal in Nova Scotia, the girl looked at me and asked, "Did you ever take a fish hook out of a puppy's mouth in Cormack?"

I said, "Yes, I did. How did you come to think I did?"

"I married the boy who carried the puppy to you," she said.

I guess that, since we had sort of a local zoo outside our home where we housed the orphan animals picked up by people all around the island, we were looked upon as doctor and nurse for all creatures wild and tame, great and small. We had a raven, a herring gull, three otters (Alf, Reggie and Joe), a mink, three lynx, a moose calf (Elsie), a bear cub (Cinderola), a lot of snowshoe hare and Johnny, the fox, our special pet. On Sundays in the summer, crowds would gather with people bringing children from as far away as Corner Brook.

We had many adventures with our animals. Selby Moss had one of the otter pierce two fingernails when he was feeding it trout through the wire one day and the otter was unable to extract its canines without our help. We pried its mouth open with a stick! Another time our otters all got away, almost on the eve of the Grand Falls Fair which we were attending with our animals. We were fortunate to retrap Alf and Reggie in trout baited box traps up by Steve's house where they were spending the days under his porch.

Joe, who was not a sibling, came back on his own. Joe was always the lazy one. He never took trout from our washtub pool by catching them. He waited and stole from Alf and Reggie, who did all the work.

We had casualties, too. Twin moose calves, whose mother had reportedly been taken by a bear, died when we were unable to stop the diarrhea with salt or strawberry extract or medication from the vet at Corner Brook. I even operated (rumen puncture) on one to relieve the bloat but the little fellow died anyway. I don't think I hastened his demise but I probably didn't help him too much.

I was also asked to solve the death of several critters on a local farm that had licked and eaten a considerable amount of ammonium nitrate and 12-24-24. Another time I was asked to cure horses with black water when they had been switched to an oats only diet when a woods camp ran out of hay. I was even asked to help with the castration of farm critters.

One of the most pleasant tasks, however, was visiting outport schools and showing lantern slides of wildlife. We'd put a sheet up on a wall and I'd gingerly insert and remove my precious slides from behind the propane heat. Schoolrooms would be packed to the doors sometimes with entire communities, save the ill and those too old to walk. This was at a time when in many other areas of Canada television was making a snowy debut!

In Cormack, Pearl and I initiated a youth group. With others, we obtained ownership of an old warehouse which we fixed up from donations given by business men on the west coast and where we held chaperoned parties and dances. The chaperons always included police protection from the Deer Lake detachment lest the experiment result in regular Saturday night knock-down drag-outs. There were the Co-op directors' meetings at the store, the church services (our United Church services were held in the schoolhouse), the times and the games of 45s in the bunkhouse once a week in winter. If you weren't too busy working there was always a lot to do in Cormack in 1955.

One interesting social event repeated quite frequently centered around the house fires of various residents. When they occurred, dozens of people were present and they invariably saved every stick of furniture, including ice boxes and kitchen ranges. Magic, you say? Maybe, but insurance sometimes came through easier than a turnip crop!

Since I had opportunity to fly over the District in aerial censusing of beaver colonies, moose and caribou, and to canoe most larger lakes and rivers and since I snowshoed or walked or drive much of the rest of the country, I was also called upon by the RCMP to help locate lost hunters. We kept a complete set of topographic sheets and most of the air photos in our office so with some knowledge from experience and with map and compass, we had a fair chance of locating people if they remained alive and cooperative. One Saturday morning when Steve and I had planned to take Constables Porter and Haddad out hunting moose, the RCMP car pulled in the yard with only Roger inside, in uniform. The hunt was cancelled, for Wayne was on one special mission, and two lost men were for Roger, Steve and me to locate, if we could. One of them was a poacher and the other a Corner Brook resident who was hurting for the first time.

We knew the country they were in and where their car was parked, but a six-inch snowfall overnight had obscured the men's tracks. Since the new snow had already fallen a foot or so, we harnessed up our rackets and started in toward Riverside Road from the hunters' vehicle parked atop Birchy Ridge. After a quarter of a mile or so we stopped and Roger fired a round from his 30-30. In a moment we heard a very faint answering shot so we took a bearing and proceeded on. It was a bright, cold day, maybe 10 degrees F. A lovely morning to cover the country; crossing lynx tracks, rabbit paths, fox and moose tracks, in the clean, new snow. Now and then crossbills or chickadees would let us know they were busy getting seeds and we soon picked up a couple of grey jays, which travelled along with us on a journey to possible food. It was a common thing to have jays picking at a moose at the same time it was being dressed out, and during winters when weasels were plentiful they, too, would visit blood puddles as you worked and sweated to panch and quarter.

The next time we stopped and fired the response was closer. We were making progress, but we stopped still again, another half-mile along and fired another shot before we got within hollering distance. When we did, it didn't take long before we came upon them. It had been more than an hour's walk, with stopping and shooting and listening and taking bearings, but the going was fairly easy. The terrain was only rolling with no steep cuts or hills, through patches of old growth birch and fir and over little bog openings. There they were; the poacher was sitting on the hair side of a front quarter of moose roasting a piece of fresh meat on a stick over a little fire. He was as calm and easy as could be.

"I knew the game warden would find me," he said as he watched us shuffle up. "I fired me last round with dat last shot!"

It was in the woods or in the country that you made friends. Sometimes in a woods camp and sometimes on a narrow trail and one time near the mouth of Harrimans Brook.

I was travelling with a summer helper, Selby Moss, and we had had a long, hard day surmounting the alder jungles about the beaver dams, making our way from the highroad down to the Humber. In fact, it was dark when we finally worked our way out of the bush to a meadow-like opening and a gravel bar in the middle of the brook. We were close to the outlet for sure, but it was too late to go further. We'd have to lay out the sleeping bags and spend the night on the bar, a safe place for a little fire and for boiling the kettle.

One can sleep soundly, even on gravel and sand when you're tired, and I was sound asleep when Moss woke me up.

"Don boy, hey," he whispered excitedly, "here's a moose here, boy."

I poked my nose out into the mosquitoes and opened an eye. There was a moose standing in the water right by our little gravel bar and in the moonlight she did look big! She was close by, too. Only a few feet from Moss. I was just pulling my head back in when old Moss reached out, grabbed a stone and heaved it at the moose. All hell broke loose! I'm telling you, it was close. He'd hit the poor moose smack in the ribs with the rock and when he did the moose took off—but towards us! Right by our heads it splashed, only missing us by a couple of feet. Well now, I was some pissed off at Selby, I want you to know, and I had some trouble getting calmed down and back to sleep. I guess if the moose had landed a hoof on my head I wouldn't have had to worry about sleep.

Soon after the first light began to creep in we boiled up and fried a bit of bacon. As we were munching away on bread and bacon, recalling the moose incident, me feeling better toward Selby now, I noticed a path going up the bank from the brook. Of course we hadn't seen it the night before since it was dark when we arrived. After we washed up the tin plates and cups and packed our gear for the trip back out of the alders and over the burn to the highroad, we walked up the path to see where it went. Lo and behold, we'd slept on rocks only a hundred yards from a log cabin! We heard voices before we got on the level to look down the path. As we approached, there were two men walking to the river's edge where a canoe was loaded, ready to take off down river to Nicholsville. This was to be my introduction to Dr. Bob Dove, who became a good friend and our family doctor, and to 'Jack' Nichols, who was also to become a good friend, a guide and a partner on trips to open country over the next several years. They had come from old Camp 37 on Adies River down to Birchy Forks and on down the Humber to Harrimans Steady cabin. A trip Bob once used to make each summer.

I dropped in to his camp on Adies one day long afterward to find no one either in the forepeak or in the cookhouse. I assumed Bob and Jack were on the river and made myself at home with a cup of tea and a biscuit. It was a warm, late afternoon in early August and I had no more than got settled when I heard someone running toward the back screen door. Suddenly in popped John, dripping wet and stark naked!

"Doc's got a big one on," he shouted and reached to the wall for the gaff. Probably he didn't want to risk tailing this one and doubtless the net Bob would have hanging from his waist was too small. Off he ran, this sparsely furred creature, to rescue the salmon, with me following him down the path to the Garden Pool. John had been cooling off taking a swim in the upper part of the pool while Bob was casting a lazy white wolf on low water down in the 'V' when thunder had struck, sending John through the alders in his birthday suit to fetch the wherewithal to land the brute. Once back at the pool, the intrepid guide waded out waist deep and waited with gaff lowered in the water while Bob eased the fish by once and then twice and, after several minutes, a third time. John lifted quickly and came to shore with the fish. This time Bob had been favoured with a tight line but on another occasion he wasn't so favoured.

One morning Bob had been raising a twelve-pounder near the warden's rock across from his camp and had tried a number of flies. Although he'd got a good look at the fish and though he had presented some spectacular flies, he didn't get the fish to take, so he left the pool to rest it for awhile. But he'd no sooner left than the warden himself stepped out on the rock from the shore, slashed the pool a couple of times, tearing the water surface into ribbons of bubbles and bang! He hooked and dragged the twelve-pounder to shore in no time flat! This was the same fisheries warden who was genuinely concerned when he had learned that one of our Natural

Resources wardens, Ron Callahan, had undergone surgery to remove 'de canister from 'is h'eyeball.' But when I arrived at Camp 37 about noon, it was Bob who was genuinely concerned and very unhappy indeed, allowing that wardens were on the river to protect fish and not to kill them! From that one hot summer's day until he died, Bob remained very unhappy with that warden. From that one hot summer's day on, that warden never fished salmon except when on holiday and never in that pool when Bob was around.

I first met Art Butt in a cabin in the woods at Gull Pond on the Halls Bay Line. In 1953, Doug Pimlott, Bob Folker and I were on our way to Sandy Drive Camp south of Badger for several months of field work amidst bears, black flies and mosquitoes, when we stopped for the night at the Gull Pond camp.

Art was a short, swarthy man with a heavy beard and a ready smile. He was, in fact, always smiling and always pleasant and full of fun.

"You boys ought to go up to Tom Joe Brook dis summer," he said. "I got a cabin dere you can stay in."

"Are there trout up Tom Joe?" I asked.

"Are there trout! Why, in de winter I went up dere and fished through de hice and de trout was so big you couldn't pull dere faces up through de holes," he said seriously.

Others had told of the time Art seized a moose and charged a sport for hunting outside the legal zone boundary in the central district, only to find that, after storing the quartered moose in a local cooler and eating steaks and roasts from the animal for several weeks, he himself had erred in placing the boundary signs up and the moose was indeed killed legally. When the magistrate ordered the moose returned and they found only two quarters remaining, both Art and the store manager responsible for the cooler expressed shock and dismay that anyone would be so bold as to steal two quarters of meat from such a public place. Well, maybe this was true and maybe it wasn't, but only Art would have known for sure, I guess.

You Can Never Step Twice In The Same River

In 1953 in Newfoundland there were still places you could put your foot down where no other human had trod, and my foot might well have made a first impression wherever I travelled there through woodland, bog or stream. Since Cormack's journey the country had indeed been opened up and developed by railroad, dams and roads but much of the Island's wilderness still held out. It had not all been conquered when I arrived.

For four months in 1953 I worked with a fellow wildlifer out of an old drive camp on Sandy Stream, which ran into the Exploits near Badger. We were in what once had been the heart of Beothuk country and our chore was to study moose, an animal introduced to Newfoundland almost a century after the passing of the Red Indian. Moose were all around us and we made as many as forty-seven moose observations in our two short observation periods on a given day. We recorded activity and behaviour a thousand times from spring to the beginning of the fall breeding season. When the blueberries ripened, we watched the geese come in to feed and saw the bears filling their bellies, putting on fat for winter. Lynx and foxes lived in this land: hare, beaver, otter, weasel and muskrats were also around us. That summer and the next were spent among the animals in essentially undisturbed parts of their habitats, only modified a little by chopping or fire. In 1954 I watched the moose in an aquatic environment on the Upper Humber, finding them at night with the aid of wet cells and spotlights. Sometimes, to study and learn, we dipped muskrats and beaver kits with a net and we shone our lights on broods of ducks before their daylight feeding. In the spring of 1955, Pearl and I moved to Cormack to live.

Back in 1946 the Newfoundland government had established an agricultural settlement scheme for veterans outside of Deer Lake in the Upper Humber Valley and named it after W.E. Cormack, who had travelled with one companion from Trinity Bay to the southwest coast and across to Bay St. George early in the nineteenth century. Small acreages were cleared, houses were built and the veterans, largely men with legends of the sea behind them and salt water in their veins, settled on the land to farm the soil, a medium almost foreign to them. The clearing had, unfortunately, removed much of what little top soil had been present and the houses were spaced far apart on by-roads while the promised ground limestone to sweeten the acid podzols took years to arrive. Cormack was a settlement of strangers without a centre, living together along nearly a hundred miles of only partially passable by-roads. It was a community with divided loyalties, politically and church-wise and except for the school it seemed a community with little heart. I first began to learn from it in 1953 and then came to be a part of it as it slowly began to knit together and grow a little, with slight improvements and many promises, until June 1958.

Our move to Cormack in 1955 was very important to both of us since it was our first regular full-time wildlife job. I was the first District Biologist for the province and the second biologist in the newly formed Wildlife Division, headed by Captain Harry Walters, formerly of the Newfoundland Ranger Force. Confederation, with its wounds still open and bleeding, was new and the Wildlife Division, like all of government, had enormous tasks ahead. Development, for better or worse, was on its way and the sterile land and water areas did not provide a high carrying capacity for most wild animals common to Newfoundland. Baselines had to be obtained quickly if humans and animals were each to be managed appropriately as forest cutting increased, human populations expanded and industrial development began.

It has been nearly forty years since Professor Hewitt asked if I would be interested in a Newfoundland goose (read moose) study. We did help establish some baseline data for wildlife back then, but more important to Pearl and me, we experienced much that was wonderful of life; much that would remain until now. Today Newfoundland has changed. There are roads where we never believed roads would go. There are hydro projects on rivers we would never have believed would be developed. There are new companies and new mills and even shopping centres where only canteens used to be. But the people remain and they haven't changed. Those first impressions made by my two feet were really nothing, though it's harder today to walk where no one ever walked before.

There are "tousands of millions" more yarns and dreams than the few related here in Newfoundland today. The puncheons and pickle barrels and the forepeaks are full of them, untold, told and retold. In fact, I'm sure the skippers are telling them right now.

So hush! Be very quiet and listen. If you're lucky and if you can see them in your mind's eye, perhaps you may just hear them yarning too.